Love on ...	... Bentley	1
Heat It U...	... P	9
...	...omas	
State Chan...	Garland	19
Blue Pommes in Killybegs	Thom Gautier	27
Uniform	Rachel Charman	43
This Woman is Dangerous	Landon Dixon	49
Splendide Girl	Courtney James	57
Lower Learning	Lynn Lake	67
Rough Justice	Beverly Langland	75
An Itch to Scratch	Tara S Nichols	89
The Deal	Sadie Wolf	99
Night at the Museum	Cyanne	109
Clean-up on Aisle Five	Elizabeth Coldwell	119
Nights in Black Satin	Sophia Valenti	127
Exemplary Employee	Charlotte Stein	137
Would You Like Fries with That?	Sommer Marsden	147
The Arresting Officer	Justine Elyot	157
Solitary Confinement	Lily Harlem	169
End of the Line	Heidi Champa	183
Naughty Christmas	Teri Fritz	193

Love on the Battlefield
by Chrissie Bentley

THE LOCAL HISTORICAL RE-ENACTMENT Society had one major problem. There was nothing to re-enact. It was true that we lived in one of the oldest townships in the state; it was true, too, that the local militia once spent three long, winter nights guarding the fort against the British. But then they found out that the fort itself wasn't even shown on the British maps, and that they'd not passed within 20 miles of the place.

So, when it came to finding any concrete battles for the local enthusiasts to re-create every summer, the only "real" confrontation in the entire town's history was a tussle between a couple of local landowners over the grazing rights on the hill, in 1863. Guns were fired (twice), blood was shed (but not because of the guns) and, when it turned out that a long dead ancestor of one of the families had moved up north from Georgia – why, for a couple of weeks that eventful summer, the town had its own Civil War.

So that, with a little embellishment of the facts and figures, is what the townsfolk elected to celebrate – the Most Northerly Engagement of the War Between the States. And every year, on July 4 weekend, the members of the Society would dust off their muskets, haul out the one cannon that had been purchased for the purpose (in case you're wondering, they took turns using it – this year, it was the Confederates' turn), and the whole town would turn out to watch. And, of course, participate.

From an historical perspective, the original "battle" was waged between no more than two families. By the time the first re-enactment was staged back in 1976, however, a neighbourly squabble had become a pitched battle, with 40, 50, men a side, and the field hospitals choking with the wretched wounded warriors. Who said history was written by the winners? When there's tourism dollars at stake, it can be rewritten by everyone.

My heart belonged to the Yankees – not through any political or even familial affiliation, mind you; that was just the side I'd been picked by. And, when the great day dawned, I put on my rented nurse's uniform, marched with the army through the town and, in the absence of any historical basis for anything we did, prepared to watch as the usual wild skirmishing began.

Which is when I was called to tend to the first of the wounded, less than 30 seconds after I arrived at the field hospital, and before half the tourists had even laid out their picnics. I'll spare you the gory details, but as the stretcher-bearers raced towards me, I heard one of them describe the wounded man as a goner, and the other one suggest they went and grabbed a beer. To toast his selfless sacrifice, no doubt.

The field hospital was exactly what it sounds like. It was in a field, and it had "hospital" painted on a sign outside. Actually, I shouldn't laugh. My fellow nurse, Miss Barnes, had gone to a lot of trouble to reconstruct what she imagined a Civil War era facility might look like – a bunch of surgical instruments from somebody's tool box, a mountain of brown-looking bandages and half a dozen shop window dummies, daubed in scarlet and missing sundry limbs. When she described our charge as the day's first "human" patient, I sincerely hoped she wouldn't try for a little extra realism in that department. As it turned out, he was going to get a lot more realism than I'd ever expected.

His torso spattered with crimson gore, Gavin Black gazed up at me. 'Am I going to live?' he asked.

I smiled and, following Miss Barnes' directions, mopped his fevered brow with a rag liberally soaked in alcohol. 'We'll do our best, soldier.' I smiled as I said it, partially out of astonishment that I'd ever been press-ganged into this pantomime (I'd always managed to wriggle out of the annual invitation in the past), but also because I knew Gavin of old, and he was far from soldierly as you could imagine.

When I was in my early teens, he was the "hip dude" in the town's only record store, the only one who knew what you were talking about when you asked for Elvis Costello and Iggy Pop records. He was the manager there now. I'd not been inside the place for years, but he was obviously doing well. I wondered if he was still considered hip by the latest wave of music-buying kids. Or whether he'd employed his own new dude to cater for the latest tastes?

I remembered other things. There'd been precious few interesting guys of my own age, and very few single ones, anywhere in town. Gavin, though he was probably six or seven years older than me, was one of the few who seemed even remotely attainable. For a time, I'd had quite the schoolgirl crush on him. I wondered if he ever realised.

The medics had already stripped off his uniform, leaving him clad in just an old vest and long-johns; I stepped back while Miss Barnes commenced encasing his entire lower torso in a spider's web of dirty bandages ('I soaked them in tea,' she'd explained earlier. 'It makes them look more authentically unsanitary').

I watched her working; then, when she announced that she was urgently required at another of the hospitals, I took over. The crafty cow was probably off to the refreshments tent for the rest of the day. You couldn't really blame her either. She was one of the motivating forces behind the entire re-enactment committee. If anyone deserved the day off, it was her.

I turned my attention to Gavin, lying grinning on the workbench. 'Dying soldiers should maybe look a little more like they're dying,' I admonished him, drilling a finger into his abdomen. He gave an involuntary 'ouch', and I smiled. 'Ouch. Yes, I'm sure a lot of them say that. So, how did you get "injured"? Just so I know where to put the most blood.'

'I was trying to reload my musket. I caught a couple of balls in the stomach.'

Oh dear. What an unfortunate turn of phrase. But I resisted the temptation to deliver the first words that came to mind ('I usually catch them in my mouth'), and pressed on. 'So, the abdomen. Messy. Very messy.' I grabbed a bottle from under the counter and uncorked it. 'This might be cold. But you're a brave soldier, you can handle it.'

Upending the bottle, a torrent of dark red liquid splashed across his bandages. 'Cheap red wine. Adds an antiseptic air to the surgery, and looks absolutely lifelike. Doesn't taste bad either.'

'I'll remember that,' he laughed; and then, 'you know, I was just remembering you as a kid. Do you still have all those records you used to buy?'

I nodded. 'Of course I do! That's a vital slice of my childhood. Half the music I still listen to today came from you.' I wondered whether I should tell him precisely why I spent so much time in the shop, just "hanging out" and listening while he rattled on about this band and that ... the first time I ever heard Blondie was when he played it. Patti Smith as well. But I thought better of it.

He continued. 'Do you remember how I was saving up to buy a keyboard? Then I was off to become a rock star? Never did get it, and then Duran Duran came along and that was all my best ideas down the toilet. I never imagined I'd still be here 20 years later.'

'Who'd have thought any of us would be?' I, too, had expected to flee before I was out of my teens; first to college and then a glittering career in some far-away city – and, to be fair, I got that far.

But I was between jobs now, and I wasn't quite sure what I wanted to do next. So I came back to the town I grew up in, and found it was just as dull as when I left it. Maybe that's why I was feeling so excited now. I didn't care that I was massaging wine-scented blood into a pile of tea-stained bandages. At least I was connecting with someone in a more meaningful way than saying 'hello' at the post office. It was also the first time I'd touched someone else's bare skin all summer.

He spoke again. 'I was just wondering; how much blood am I actually meant to be losing here?'

I looked down. The bottle was half empty. 'Oh, just a couple of pints for now, but it'll keep coming. You'll probably be dead by the end of the day.' I paused as my eyes travelled down his body. 'Although, I'm wondering if your wound is the only thing that's draining it?'

I saw his eyes follow mine, and his face turned as scarlet as the blood. Straining against the fabric of his red-stained longjohns, a fat, one-eyed helmet peeking over the edge of the cotton waistband, he was nursing the biggest hard-on I'd seen in years – and certainly the biggest that I'd never even noticed.

He spluttered an apology, but I put my fingers to his lips. 'Don't try to speak. You're dangerously weak and any unnecessary exertion could easily finish you off.' I lay the palm of my hand an inch or so over the bulge, could feel the heat radiating out of it. 'Massive blood loss. Dangerously overheated. I have to try and find a way of staunching the flow.'

Gently, I pulled his underpants away, and his cock leaped to attention, as fat as that first glimpse had promised, and – as my friend Lisa sometimes liked to say, 'long enough to tickle your tonsils'. I looked around – the tent was still empty, and the only voices in earshot sounded some way away. 'Everyone's off with the fighting. This tent's more for show,' I mused. 'All the other casualties will be down there, with Dr Ronstadt.'

'Lucky for me,' he smiled, and I grinned back. 'Lucky for me, as well.' I stroked his cock, and squeezed as it twitched in response. 'Civil War medicine is usually so boring.'

My hand was tight around him, squeezing and easing the pressure of my grip, but never doing more than that. The thought of somebody wandering past and seeing us was alive in my mind, but that was only a part of it. I just wanted to savour the moment ... squeeze and release ... squeeze and release ... squeeze and release.

He reached a hand up to touch my breasts, but I stepped to one side, just out of reach. 'Maybe when you're feeling better.' Squeeze.

'I'm feeling pretty good right now.'

Release. 'So you say.' Squeeze. 'But I say there's still room for improvement.' Release. My hand relaxed and, where once I had gripped him firmly in my fist, now the lightest of fingers cradled him. 'Definitely room for improvement.'

Squeeze ... and the faintest bubble of moisture appeared from the slit at the tip. Release; and I pressed my thumb against the droplet, smeared it roughly over his helmet. I glanced over and saw his eyes fixed on mine, their expectant glitter begging me to lean forward, to take him in my mouth. I wanted to as well, but I resisted the temptation. For now. Rather, I watched him watching me, then heard him moan slightly as my hand jerked up suddenly, milking the pre-come from deep within.

Then, with the end of his cock now glistening with moisture, I leaned forward, to blow gently onto the crest. He gasped, and I looked across at him. He really did have beautiful eyes.

'Is everything OK?' I asked. 'Do you have everything

you need?'

'I need to be inside you. I want to feel myself inside you ... inside your mouth.'

I adopted what I hoped was my most officious tone. 'I thought that might be it. But I still don't think you're ready.' I straightened up, but this time, as I enclosed his stiffness in a tight fist, there was none of the gentle tease of before. Instead, my hand was a blur, massaging his shaft, jerking him so hard that it seemed no more than a minute before I felt his balls begin to tense, and a low growl forming in his throat. 'I'm coming! Oh fuck, I'm coming!'

I did my best to control my own excitement. 'I know,' I said calmly. 'And now I want to ...' – but before I'd even finished my sentence, before I had a chance to tell him how desperately I wanted to feel his hot come on my face and lips, he erupted, a long, hard, boiling geyser of white erupting out of him, arching over the bandages to spatter his chest.

More hit my hand; more still splashed the stretcher beneath him. It felt as though it would never stop – even as my grip relaxed, I could still feel the frenzied jolts as his balls emptied themselves. But finally the flood subsided; his cock was softening already.

I bent down and raised it to my mouth, gently enclosing the head between my lips as I sucked the last drops of come out of him, his salty softness so deep inside my mouth that my nose was pressing into his belly. But finally I released him, straightened up and adjusted my uniform.

'I really think you're on the road to recovery, soldier boy,' I laughed, as I picked up the come and wine-soaked bandages, and balled them into the garbage. 'So it's time to reload your musket again. But this time, let's find somewhere else to put the balls.' Then my mouth closed over one-half of his scrotum, and I felt him beginning to stiffen again. And I knew that this was one re-enactment that I was really going to enjoy.

Heat It Up
by Shashauna P Thomas

WHEN IT COMES TO what turns people on sexually, everyone has their own kinks. Things that are guaranteed to rev them up from zero to 90 in seconds. For some it's the sight of leather bondage and handcuffs, while others love pedicures in high-heeled shoes. Everyone has fetishes whether they want to admit it or not. I bet if more people were open with their sexual hot buttons they'd find their fetishes are more common than they think. Take mine for example. I love a man in uniform. For me there's always been something hot and rugged about a man dressed up in the standardised uniform of their profession that seems to make them even more appealing. Almost like the generic uniform tries to cage their innate masculinity and emphasises them instead. Mailmen, bus drivers, officers, doctors, surgeons, and paramedics all get my feminine juices flowing. However, my reaction to all of them combined is nothing compared to what happens when I see a man in what I consider the definitive panty soakers ... the fireman uniform.

It doesn't matter if they're suited up in hard hats with matching yellow and black jumpers or if they're wearing the plain dark pants, light short sleeve shirt or dark coloured T-shirt with the fire department initials on the back. Either way I want to lick them from head to toe. Grab one by his suspenders, hop on him, wrap my legs around his waist, and proceed to play tonsil hockey for a few hours. I love firemen. One of the first things that I noticed about my apartment when I first moved in was that it was directly across the street from a firehouse. The noise of the area in addition to the noise of the fire engines was one of the reasons the apartment was so affordable. Others might not like living so close to a firehouse, but I personally consider it a perk.

Looking out the window every day and getting glimpses of the strong, muscle-bound men was slowly driving me insane. Watching them wash down the engine, pile into the engine while racing off to respond to a call or just hanging around the firehouse often had me sitting at my bedroom window salivating like a starving dog with a bowl full of bones directly just out of reach. I hadn't even met them yet and they were affecting my sanity along with my libido. It was pure insanity that spurred me into action. With a tin full of homemade chocolate chip cookies I made my way across the street to the firehouse. I had no idea how myself or my cookies would be received, as it was the first time I'd ever been inside a firehouse. I had no idea if they had any rules about civilians being around but I figured there was only one way to find out.

Lucky for me the bunch of guys I first met were extremely friendly and welcoming to a young attractive woman walking right in with a bunch of cookies. It just so happened that the first one I walked into was the chief. He was a nice older man who, off the bat, made me feel welcomed and reminded me of my father. The chief said he didn't mind me coming around as long as I promised not to get in the way when a call came in. All the guys were nice, friendly and, in general, good guys to hang around with. I started coming at different times to meet the other guys who worked different shifts. Some were hot and some were average but in their uniforms, none were disappointing.

I enjoyed hanging out at the firehouse with the guys. They enjoyed my company as much as they enjoyed my cooking skills. I found out that the guys took turns cooking, and some were better at it than others, so my little contributions to the menu were always welcomed. Even the chief enjoyed my cooking while teasing me that I was trying to fatten them up. I'd make them cookies, brownies, fried chicken, meatloaf, and a number of other things. I came so often I knew each and every one who worked there. Who was married, who had a girlfriend, who was single, who had kids, who didn't, who was a comedian, and who was serious. Mark was the serious one.

Mark was the strong silent type. He was always polite, and didn't say much to me, but the way I'd catch him looking at me when I was in the firehouse told a totally different story. In regards to size, Mark was the biggest firemen there in height and muscles. I knew he was intelligent from the short talks we managed to have but mostly from conversations he had with others that I overheard. Mark had been a fire-fighter longer than most in the station and, from what I've gathered, had seen more fires then the rest of them. When he'd strut around the station that experience exuded in everything he did along with restrained power that seemed to roll off him in waves. Even with his massive size he reminded me of a graceful lion prowling his territory. He was the physical embodiment of every single fireman fantasy I'd ever had. It didn't matter that I knew him the least out of all the firemen; I knew I wanted him and no one else would do. My only problem was how to get my hands on him. Lucky for me, an opportunity unexpectedly presented itself.

It had been a really busy week at work. I barely made it home for a quick nap, shower, and a change of clothes most nights, much less had the time to cook something and bring it over to the boys in the firehouse. That Friday night I had just enough energy to make a pan of lasagne before I collapsed in the bed from exhaustion. Saturday night I had planned a much deserved evening out with the girls so I woke up early Saturday afternoon and treated myself to a spa day. I spent the whole day pampering myself. With my hair and nails done, wearing the new outfit I'd bought, I was more than ready for a number of drinks combined with an evening of dancing and flirting with friends at a club. On my way out I grabbed the lasagne deciding to drop it off at the station on my way out. It was summer so I wasn't cold in the short black skirt, tank top, and heels. As usual, the big bay doors were open, the lights were on, and one of the engines was parked half in and half out. The only thing out of the ordinary was how quiet it seemed inside. Even though I'd been coming there for months I still hadn't had a tour so I had no idea where everyone was. The only sounds I heard were the clicking of my heels on the pavement and a TV on low. I figured it was coming from the small lounge I'd seen off from the dining room.

As I leaned against the cracked door I said, 'Hello?' The only light in the room was coming from the glowing television, illuminating the lone figure sitting on the coach facing away from the door. It was still too dark to see who it was, but I could see he had turned around and was now facing me in the open doorway. 'Hey, where is everyone?'

'Oh hey. A couple of the guys went out shopping for groceries. The rest are sleeping upstairs.' The deep timbre of the voice told me who it was before he reached over to the lamp on the side table. With the dim lighting I now saw Mark standing in front of the couch facing me with a can of soda in his hand. His button down uniform shirt undone, exposing the white wife-beater underneath cascading over rippling abs.

'I didn't think you guys ever slept.' I replied, well practised in hiding the butterflies in my stomach that he never failed to provoke. 'I just stopped by to say hello and to bring you boys some of my lasagne.' He didn't respond, just stood there staring at me with his dark intense eyes. He's always quiet but I'd never seen such an intense look from him before. It was making me more nervous by the minute. 'Should I just leave it on the table or should I put it in the fridge?'

'You can leave it on the table. I'm sure when the guys get back they'll want some. That is if the guys upstairs don't finish it off first.' He replied with a smirk. I nodded and made my way next door to the eating area. This part of the firehouse I was well familiar with. After placing the tin in the middle of the table I turned around and almost jumped to find Mark leaning in the doorway watching me. I hadn't expected him to follow me, and he was so silent I hadn't heard him. 'Do you usually make lasagne dressed like that?' It was then that I realised this was the first time he'd seen me dressed up. I usually came to the firehouse dressed casual. No wonder the fire I normally see in his eyes seemed to be raging tonight.

Shaking my head no, I replied, 'Not exactly. I'd been so busy I really hadn't had the time to bring you guys any of my cooking so I made a lasagne last night. Thought I'd come by, visit for a while, and drop it off on my way out for the night.'

'Well as you can see everyone's either asleep or not here ...' He said as he strolled into the room closing in on me and my personal space. '... but you could visit with me for a while if you're interested.' His voice getting deeper by the moment.

'I think I can manage to spare a few moments.' Smiling deviously as I brushed past him and on my way out of the eating area and back to the main bay. Stopping in front of the huge red fire-truck an idea began to form. So I turned around to face Mark as he closed in on me once again. 'You know, of all the times I've been here I still haven't received the grand tour. How about you give me my own private tour starting with the engine?'

'Sure.' He replied and proceeded to show me around the fire-truck. He took his time pointing to different parts of the truck explaining what they were called and their function. It was interesting and any other time I would've been spellbound and asking ten million questions but the subtle little touches he managed to casually slip in kept distracting me. The feel of his hands on my exposed skin frazzled my brain and nodding my head seemed to be all I could manage.

Then glancing up at the front of the fire-truck behind the cab, I managed to ask, 'Can we see the inside?'

'You sure you can get up there in those heels?' Mark chuckled.

'You'd be surprised what I'm capable of doing in these heels.'

'Pleasantly surprised no doubt.' He replied as he helped me up onto the silver steps into the truck by conveniently placing his hands on my thighs and he easily lifted me up to the first step. I knew the inside of the truck would be cramped with a low ceiling, but once one sits down on the dark bench seating you can see that there is enough headroom as well as enough space for a number of firemen to fit when responding to a call. We sat on opposite sides facing each other as he continued to explain what everything was. Leaning back with his arm up in the open window slot, his eyes continued to blaze with interest as they roamed up and down my body. When he finally ran out of things to explain I decided to take advantage of the quiet and finally make my move. With my stomach fluttering I knew it was now or never.

'I know you're attracted to me, Mark, as I am to you. So tell me why this is the most time we've spent together and why this is the first time you seem ready to give me the time of day?' I asked in a sulky voice as I slowly began running my hands along my body.

'It was for your own good. You're a small petite little thing, and I'm a big guy who likes to get really rough with my partners. I still don't know if you're able to handle me, but you make it incredibly hard to deny what I want to do to you.' He reached down and adjusted his pants making room for the enormous erection begging for attention.

'Oh I've just begun to make it hard for you, Mark. Why don't you let me worry about what I can and can't handle while you worry about making sure you satisfy my needs.' Slowly spreading my legs wide enough for him to see up my skirt as my hand slowly inched up the inside of my leg. I began rubbing myself through my black thong; moaning as I imagined it was his big hands that were playing between my legs. Slipping two fingers under the thong rubbing my juices into my engorged clit. The only sounds were my elevated breathing and my hand moving in my moisture.

'Show me what you like, baby. Use your other hand to play with your nipple.' Keeping in mind that at any moment one of the guys sleeping upstairs could come down, I tried to keep my moans as low as possible. Lifting my hand I pulled my fitted tank up exposing my bare breast to his eyes. Mark sat there across from me with his hands balled into tight fists as I masturbated for him. The look on his face, the tension radiating throughout his body, and the lust burning in his eyes had me so turned on I felt my orgasm beginning to build a lot sooner than expected. 'That's it, baby. Come for me. Let me see you come apart.' His voice was all I needed to push me over the edge. I bit my bottom lip muffling the sound of my release. I was still trying to get my breathing under control when he said in a deep commanding voice 'Come over here.'

Standing on shaking legs and hunching over slightly I walked the few steps to stand directly in front of him. With one hand he took mine and began to suck the juices off my fingers while the other reached under my skirt. With a strong grip on my thong he tugged hard, ripping it off me. He leaned forward and roughly consumed my nipples. Alternating between sucking and biting. His hands massaging my butt as mine held his shoulders were the only things keeping me upright; my legs felt like jelly. Suddenly he released my breast and flipped me around before pulling me down onto his lap. Spreading my legs open so I straddled his thighs. He played with my nipples as I began grinding on his dick through his pants. I couldn't remember a time I'd ever been so aroused. The man drove me insane, and the only thing that would've been hotter was if he were wearing his yellow jumpsuit and hard hat. Oh the things I'd imagined doing to him with those suspenders.

'Undo my pants.' Even though his voice was a whisper in my ear I heard the command in his voice. Causing me to shiver as I reached between our legs and undid his zipper. Somehow he managed to reach into his pocket and pull out his wallet. Inside his wallet he pulled out a condom then handed it to me then slouched down as he commanded me to put it on. Driving myself crazy as much as him, I took my time rolling it down, paying close attention to the base of his shaft, and letting my fingers graze his balls once the condom was all the way on. 'Oh, you're so going to get it.'

'I'm on fire! I ... I need you to squelch the burning inside. You think you ... you can handle it?' I managed to get out as he rubbed the head of his shaft slowly back and forth over my sensitive clit.

'My pleasure.' He grunted as he positioned his head at my opening and began slowly thrusting. Not stopping until he was fully seated inside me. I began riding him following the pace he set. The feel of him deep inside had me moaning and digging my nails into his arms. His hands continued tweaking my nipples, adding another intense sensation to the numerous others coursing through my body. I felt his mouth nibble at my ear, neck and shoulder. Our slow pace began to increase to a fast and pounding one. His shaft managed to constantly hit my g-spot at just the right angle and I began to moan louder not caring if anyone heard me. Sooner than I imagined I felt my second orgasm begin to build as my inner walls started to contract around him as he pistoned away inside me. Then he squeezed my nipples causing my orgasm to crest. As I came apart on his lap he continued pounding away. Then he managed to get us both down on the floor on our knees, placing my hands on the bench and his on my hips not missing a beat. As my orgasm began to ease, another unexpected orgasm began driving me right back to my peak. I gripped and screamed into the bench seat as my hot fire-fighter grunted as he continued to fuck me from behind, now caught in the throes of his own orgasm. Feeling him come inside the condom and his fingers grip my hips so hard I was sure I'd have imprints later made my third and final orgasm last longer than the others. It was amazing.

By the time we were finished in the fire-truck it was way too late to meet the girls at the bar. I was much too relaxed and sated to go anywhere but home anyway. Luckily we didn't run into any of the others as we exited the truck. I gave him a quick kiss turning to leave. Remembering the lasagne was still cool from the fridge, I said over my shoulder, 'Don't forget to heat it up.'

'I think we already did.' He replied. I heard the smile in his voice and knew he understood what I was referring to just as I knew what he was. To say I slept like a baby that night would be an understatement. I didn't know if we were loud enough to wake anyone up, but at the time I really couldn't care less if they stood in the doorway and watched us. It was so good I still to this day could care less if we were caught and watched. If I was completely honest the thought itself makes me hot all over again. I don't exactly remember what happened to the remains of my thong but I suspect Mark took them. I highly doubt he left them in the truck for the boys to find.

I continued to come by the firehouse to hang as well as bring the boys more of my cooking and no one gave any indication they knew what happened. Mark has been much friendlier towards me and we've hooked up a couple more times since at my place. Each time it seems better than the last, which is hard to fathom as that night in the fire-truck was absolutely incredible. Now that he knows about my uniform fetish he has promised me another private tour of the firehouse. I'm not sure how he's going to manage it without any of the other guys finding out, but I told him as long as he wore his hard hat and suspenders, I was game for anything. I really do love a man in uniform and enjoy doing my part to support the local fire department.

State Champs
by Garland

I SAW HIM AS soon as I stepped off the bus. Our eyes met across the parking lot and for one brief moment there was no one else in the world but the two of us. As he helped his band mates unload their bus he never stopped looking at me. He was incredibly handsome.

Why did he have to be enrolled in a rival college? The college that was our band's fiercest competition for the state championship no less. It's my tragic flaw, always falling for the wrong guy. They're either married, gay, involved with someone else, batshit crazy, teachers or assholes.

As we unloaded the gear from our bus I watched him grow smaller and smaller as he and his mates went to get settled in their rooms. I couldn't help but blush a little as he turned and watched every move I was making.

That night after my roommates had drifted off to sleep, I lay in bed and fingered myself as I thought about the rival stranger. I couldn't believe I was actually fantasizing about a guy I saw across a parking lot. A guy whose name I didn't even know. Guess it's been too damn long since I'd gotten some dick. Or at least some really good dick. Though, of course, I had no clue if he knew how to use his.

It was so hard to keep silent and stifle my euphoric screams as the orgasm ripped through my body. My back arched and I practically levitated off the bed as I jammed my fingers deeper into my pussy.

I couldn't believe it. I had actually become that girl. The

kind who falls in lust with a stranger and then spends every single goddamn moment thinking about him.

The next day I wandered the grounds aimlessly. I told myself I was just preparing myself for the preliminary round later that day but I knew that was bullshit. I was searching for him. I had no clue what I'd do if and when I found him but I had some creative ideas.

'Slow down, girl,' I cautioned myself. 'You don't know anything about this guy. He could have a girlfriend. Be into dudes. Be an asshole. A psycho.'

A heavy sigh caused my shoulders to rise and fall. Damn it! Why did he have to be so friggin' hot?

'This is ridiculous,' I finally found my voice of reason. 'You are getting a Master's. Quit acting like a character on *The CW*.'

The voice of reason was right. Turning a corner I was ready to give up on my idiotic quest when I saw him. Screw that stupid voice of reason! He was even hotter close up!

He was with his clarinet playing buddy less than ten feet away. Subtly I hid behind the judge's booth and watched him. My pussy was salivating with wanton desire.

He was wearing his uniform pants, a heavy maroon colour and no shirt. The uniform's suspenders wrapped themselves around his broad shoulders and clung to his muscular back. His bass drum rested against his stomach, strap hugging his neck. I wished my arms were around his neck. I never thought a man in a band uniform could get me so excited!

My heart rate increased and my stomach knotted itself into a tight pretzel of nerves as I watched him beat his drum. I've always been attracted to drummers. With all that natural rhythm they're almost always great in bed.

As I watched him my fingers found their way into my sweat pants and played with my pussy. My breathing increased as my nails got tangled in my moist dark curls. My knees buckled as I imagined pulling down his heavy wool pants and sucking his dick as he beat his drum.

My knees buckled and a small moan escaped me. Holding on to the wall I fingered myself harder. I was so close. Crying out louder than I intended, I came all over my fingers.

'What was that?' The drummer's friend asked putting down the clarinet.

'I don't know,' the drummer replied gazing towards the judge's booth.

Quickly I ducked my head out of sight and kicked myself. Damn it! Talk about having no self-control. I wondered if they had seen.

'I don't see anything,' the drummer finally said.

Thank God. I breathed a sigh of relief.

'Come on, man, let's go. I wanna shower and get out of this hot uniform,' the clarinet player said.

'Yeah. It's hot as hell out here.'

'Why do they have state in the middle of summer?' The clarinet player asked. 'And why can't they give us some summer-friendly uniforms?'

'To torture us,' the drummer laughed. I could hear the smirk on his lips and that turned me on. I wondered if he'd smirk as he fucked me. I don't know why but he seemed like the type who would. You know the type. The kind of guy who knows he's a good fuck and gets that cocky grin all over his lips as he makes your pussy squirt.

Glued to the wall I held my breath and listened to them walk away. Listening intently I waited until their footsteps were a distant memory before I dared to breathe.

Peeking around the corner I finally relaxed. They were gone. Now it was time to go back to my room, take a very cold shower and get ready for the prelims.

Turning I screamed and nearly fell backwards. The drummer was less than an inch from me. Damn! How was he able to sneak up on me? Boy was light on his feet.

With unbelievable quickness his arm wrapped around

me and pulled me tight against him. Fuck! I can't tell you what a thrill it was to be pressed against him. His nude chest against my cotton T-shirt. Gasping I breathed in his scent and felt my pussy lips stir to life.

'Sorry,' he said with a grin that would put the Cheshire Cat to shame. 'Didn't mean to scare you.'

'You didn't,' I badly lied.

'Did you like watching me?' He asked with a cocky voice.

'I wasn't watching you,' I said feeling my cheeks burn with an embarrassed fever.

'Bullshit. I heard you. It sounded like you enjoyed what you saw.' A surprised squeak spilled over my lips as his hand got lost inside my sweats and rested on my pussy. 'Feels like you enjoyed it too.'

I wanted to slap him. I should have slapped him and walked away. Instead I just stood there, eyes half-closed, enjoying the feel of his large hand against my sensitive flesh.

'You like that?' He asked rubbing my pussy with his palm.

'Mmmmm ...' I moaned feeling his bulge quiver and wake up beneath the heavy fabric of his pants.

'I was hoping we'd get to meet since I saw you yesterday,' he whispered sending tingles down my spine despite the blistering heat. 'I'm Zak.'

'LaRhondra,' I moaned.

'Pretty name,' he complimented. 'For a pretty girl.'

Slowly his lips pressed against mine. They were so soft. Moist. Sweet as honey. His tongue snuck out of his mouth and pried my lips opened. He entered my mouth and our tongues joined together in a sensual waltz.

All too soon we parted.

'See you later,' he said winking, pinching my pussy lips as he removed his hand. 'Good luck this afternoon.'

Backing away he licked my pussy juices off the palm of

his hand before turning and walking back to his room. My eyes were glued on the way his pants clutched his ass. I wished I could clutch it. I still don't know how I kept myself from running after him, throwing him on the ground and riding his dick 'til dawn. Guess I have more self-control then I thought.

Later at the prelims it was hard as hell to concentrate on directing the band. Zak was standing on the sidelines, leaning lazily against the bleachers, watching everything I did. I was sweating more than usual. My heart was pumping so hard I was scared it would stop.

Damn, I thought. Maybe this guy is a wizard 'cause he's definitely cast some kind of spell on me.

After my band was done, I wanted to stick around and watch Zak but I didn't trust myself. What if I was overcome with lust, desire or whatever the hell you want to call it and I ran onto the field and fucked him? I'm pretty sure my band wouldn't advance to the final round.

I had gotten as far away from the action as I could. Still clad in my band uniform, I was leaning against the fence and sipping some water. Taking off my hat, I threw it to the ground and ran my hands through my long braids. Looking at the tall mountains rise up and slice the sky, I contemplated the best way to avoid seeing Zak for the rest of the competition.

'I liked your band's routine,' Zak's voice made me jump.

Goddamn it! So much for not seeing him.

'Thanks,' I said quickly, trying to avoid looking at him.

'You're a very good drum major. A lot better than ours. He has no rhythm or sense of timing.'

'Thank you. I hope to be a conductor,' I answered trying to remember how to breathe.

'I bet you'll be a great conductor,' Zak said making me blush.

'You don't even know me,' I flirted fingering the shiny

brass buttons of his uniform.

'I'd like to,' he responded.

Silence, thick with sexual tension hung between us. We stared at each other, never taking our eyes from each other.

It all happened so fast. The raw sexual desire overpowered us and like animals we sprang. Our arms locked around each other, fingers digging into our uniforms' heavy fabric.

Zak tore open my jacket, freeing my breasts. Moaning, I closed my eyes as he swallowed them whole. His teeth gently tugged on my dark mocha-coloured nipples. As he sucked on my breasts I undid the buttons of his jacket and caressed his hairy chest.

His tongue slowly made its way down my stomach. It swirled around my navel and tickled my quivering flesh. Like a wild animal he tore open my pants and pushed them down around my ankles. I was all set for him to snack on my snatch but he had other plans.

Picking up my helmet Zak placed my hands high above my head and secured them to the chain-link fence with the helmet's strap. It was then I noticed the large bass drum mallet on the ground. My heart thudded in anticipation.

With a mischievous wink he picked up the mallet and ran the soft padded head against my skin as he kissed my lips softly. Small moans of approval escaped my mouth and entered his as Zak hit the mallet against my breasts. I fingered the hot leather strap as the mallet travelled over my stomach, making my sensitive flesh quiver with erotic earthquakes.

My knees buckled as soon as the head made contact with my moist curls. He hit my pussy like it was his drum; making it grow wetter. Zak torturously rubbed my pussy lips before easily slipping the mallet inside me.

'Oh,' I gasped out as I felt my pussy stretch to accommodate the massive head.

Zak fucked me with slow even strokes. Biting my lips I

moaned. My stomach tingled. My pulse raced.

Zak undid his pants, turned around, spread his delicious ass and pushed against the end of the mallet. I watched, totally turned on, as the mallet entered him. This guy was as kinky as me! I loved it.

His ass was pressed right up against my pussy. He slowly moved his ass back and forth. I watched hypnotised as he fucked himself on the mallet.

'Fuck me,' he moaned, stroking his dick.

Finding my rhythm I fucked him like he was my bitch. His ass cheeks jiggled like Jell-O as I picked up speed. The helmet beat against the chain-link fence harder and harder. Our moans were in perfect harmony.

When his ass had had its fill he turned around, removed the mallet and ate my pussy like a starving man. Shoving his tongue deep inside me, he tickled my clit as he lapped up all my juices.

My pussy was overcome with passion. With an orgasmic tug I broke the helmet's strap. Surprising both of us I grabbed hold of his jacket and shoved him against the fence. Zak laughed as I kissed him and squeezed his balls.

Slowly I slid down Zak's body, nails tickling his flesh. My uniform, still around my ankles, acted as a cushion as I got on my knees, opened wide and swallowed him whole. Zak's fat cock fit nicely in my mouth. Squeezing his large balls I bobbed my head back and forth. His hands got tangled in my braids and gently tugged them.

'I wanna fuck you,' he whispered.

'Good,' I said stroking his slippery cock. ''Cause I want you to fuck me.'

Placing his hands on my jacket he jerked me to my feet. My pants sagged lower and got tangled around my ankles. Kissing me I slammed him against the fence. Guiding his cock into my pussy I moaned with contentment. Kissing me, he took control and slammed me against the fence before slamming his cock in and out of me.

Wrapping my legs around his waist, he fucked me harder. The chain-link rattled. I was scared we'd tip the damn fence over. As we kissed I moaned madly into his mouth.

As we were fucking, Zak's pants got tangled around his ankles. Losing his balance he fell on his back. His dick was still in me and I rode him like he was a prized stallion.

Laughing and smiling cockily like I knew he would, his hands squeezed my breasts, then his fingers flicked against my clit.

Wrapping his arms around my neck he pulled my mouth to his and kissed me with a fire I didn't even know a man could possess. Flipping me onto my back, his dick pumped into me like a jackhammer. His balls slapped against me. Clutching his uniform-clad shoulders I screamed as he came deep in my pussy.

'Goddamn,' he moaned. 'That was intense.'

'Yeah,' I agreed pecking his lips. 'I love white boy dick.'

Laughing he rolled off me and tweaked my hard nipples. 'Good. 'Cause I've always been a chocoholic. Well,' he said pulling up his pants and buttoning his jacket. 'See ya.'

Lying there in my sweaty uniform I watched him disappear. My band was placed first. I never saw Zak again. I didn't expect to. It was a casual fuck. Nothing more. We both knew it and that's what we wanted. But I never forgot that incredible fuck he gave me.

Blue Pommes in Killybegs
by Thom Gautier

I FIRST SAW HER bringing up the rear in the bridal procession and I was hooked. She was the last bridesmaid and the tallest one, in a strapless ivory gown with a slanted skirt line cut diagonally just below her knees. An acquaintance insisted that I'd met her the night before at the pre-wedding fete. 'Not a chance,' I said, 'I would have remembered that aggressive gait.'

This was in Ireland, a second cousin's wedding, an event I'd decided to fly across the Atlantic to attend, partly to escape a half-assed relationship I was in back home. I was in a damp church in a hilly place called Killybegs and I was infatuated from afar.

Besides being taller, she was older by a few years than the other three bridesmaids. Even in the dim church lighting, her lean, broad shoulders had a rosy glow to them. Not a *blushing* glow but burnished, like the tint from the pink-stained glass window. Up at the altar, she was poised and distinctive and her height and mature demeanour seemed ill-suited to the prim ivory bridesmaid dress.

Much later, in the brighter lit catering hall, I caught sight of her animated hazel-coloured eyes as she yakked it up with men and women alike. She had short reddish brown hair which she frequently swatted from her forehead with an indifference that I found sexy.

I finally struck up a conversation with her after the wedding dinner. As the band was on a break, the dance-floor was empty and she and I were alone, hidden behind the bandstand.

'I like your ... *uniform*,' I said.

'Pardon?' she asked. Puzzled, she gazed down at her dress. '*This*? This is a uniform is it?'

'Well, three ladies in the same dress,' I said. 'What is it if not a uniform?'

'Um, well, it's a special order. Custom. It's what it is. It's – well, it's a *fecking* dress,' she said, winking, her combative tone offset by a friendly glint in her eyes. There were no rings on her fingers but I wondered about a boyfriend. As we chatted, she let slip a sly smile, and as she sipped from her pint glass, her eyes peered over the rim of the glass both suspiciously and flirtatiously. Her long fingers grasped the glass sweetly.

'Doesn't matter that it's a dress,' I said. 'Meter maids wear dresses, and they're still *uniforms*.'

She dismissed my meter maid point. 'We don't have meter maids in Ireland,' she said, which I knew had to be a lie. 'There are meters in Donegal,' I said, 'so there must be maids.' She picked my brain about where I was from in the States, who I knew from the wedding, whether I always "harassed" beleaguered bridesmaids about their dresses like this. I told her she seemed anything but "beleaguered", by my harassment. She offered me a sip of her dark beer and I took it and drank slowly, returning her contented gaze as I sipped.

We chatted with warm humour and the warmth between us seemed to increase with every word.

She quizzed me about whether I wore a uniform in my chosen profession. 'I'm a graphic artist,' I told her. 'A painter's smock is my uniform.'

I could tell she was taking her time with me, as if to gauge whether I'd come to this wedding alone, and the longer she took in questioning me, the more I sensed *she*'d come alone.

'Listen, Yank, a uniform is something a person who wears it isn't really keen to. I didn't mind this dress at all. It's smashing by comparison to the duds I've worn for other weddings. Now, you want to talk uniforms, I've a secondary school uniform hanging in my wardrobe,' she said. 'Get this – nine years on, she still fits me. I used to hate wearing it but now that she still fits, I think, well there's a *proper* uniform.'

Her personifying her uniform as "she" was more than sexy. It suggested someone with a rich fantasy life and I felt privileged to be let in on her little obsession. I imagined her with the uniform on.

'Friday last. Before a full-length mirror. Should I tell you how jealous some of my former schoolmates were when they found out it still fit me?'

As she repeated her claims about her old school uniform fitting her, I studied her from her hairline to toe. Her waistline was slim. The temptation to cup my hands around that satin-wrapped waist was so strong that I "borrowed" another sip of her pint to distract me from my desire. For all her height and her long limbs, she was slender. Her thin lips were cherry red, freshly daubed with lipstick. Still, I was dubious about the uniform claim, and I told her so.

'You don't believe it still fits me?' she asked, 'Ah, sceptical Yank.'

'Tell me more about this infamous uniform. This *she* that still fits you.'

'Oh you'd love the sight of it. Kilt of various blues, that's now four inches above my knees, grey shirt with tie, light navy blazer, black tights and pommes.'

'*Pommes?*'

An older woman came round the bandstand to fetch her for the cake-cutting and as the woman tried to pull "Geraldine" aside, she clutched her pint glass and wagged a finger at me. 'You could do with a uniform yourself, Yank.' She pointed at my sports jacket and shoes.

The older woman had her by the arm. 'I promise to

bring her back,' the friend said to me, and I felt erotically taken care of by this older woman's promise. The two vanished for a moment and then my newfound friend's head reappeared behind the bandstand, her sweeps of reddish brown hair tousled over her eyes. 'Only kidding about the duds, Yank, you put these local boys to shame with those threads. Don't you dare disappear.'

I needed to do some recon on this woman, and while the cake was cut, I had a cousin fill me in. 'She's no shrinking violet,' he told me.

'No shit,' I said.

Her name was indeed Geraldine. Gerri. Just back from a year and a half tending a bar in Scotland. Going to school to be a math teacher. The school reference reminded me of her uniform claim. Long legs like hers, I thought, if her claim is true: what a sight she'd be in that.

'Is she *single*?' I asked.

'Complicated,' my cousin answered. 'They're both not going together and also still have something. He's with her and he's also stalking her.'

'Sounds a little nuts,' I said, 'but whose relationships aren't?'

My cousin drew a photo from his wallet – a local newspaper clipping featuring a burly rugby player in a green and gold uniform. My cousin explained to me what league this guy was in and – not knowing or caring a thing about Irish football – I hardly paid attention.

'Cute gym shorts,' I said with American condescension. 'Her football champ's not *here* is he?' He wasn't.

'Cute uniform,' I said, handing the clipping back. Then I asked him did he know what "pommes" are.

'French apples?' he answered.

The drizzling rain was refreshing and the cold night air wakened me. The wedding guests were dispersing amid plans to converge on a nearby after-hours club. I was indifferent: I knew what I wanted, and I sensed from the electricity we'd charged up behind the bandstand, I knew what Gerri wanted. And *how*.

I didn't see Gerri anywhere. And just as I leapt on a crate to survey the crowd, I felt a poke in my hips. 'Going to turn into an American army general and bark orders?' she asked me. I told her I could do as much, 'I have medals at home.' When I stepped down, she and I almost hugged, as if this were a reunion and we'd been separated for years rather than 40 minutes.

'Let's have your name now,' she asked me, as if she were asking me to surrender my gun. When I told her my name was Thom, she started calling me *Tommy*.

'*Thom*,' I insisted, grinning.

Gerri revealed to the bridesmaids how 'Tommy here' had described their dresses as 'uniforms'.

'Apologies,' I said, 'you are all too glamorous for the word "uniform" – that dress is anything but.'

'That so?' Geraldine said. 'Don't you love a man who stands by his opinions? You'd fold under pressure quickly, you would.'

The bridesmaids tried to side with me, arguing with Gerri that there was "a uniform aspect" to the dresses. Slants of light from the catering hall light up Gerri's eyes, and cast her wide but small-boned nose in pretty relief. I studied the petal-folds of the corsage that dangled limply from her wrist. I wanted her alone. And now. As I discussed the "dress issue" with the gaggle of girls, Geraldine held my gaze, possessively, arching her eyebrows to indicate I was impressing her with how much attention these younger bridesmaids were paying me. She grabbed on to my right arm like she was claiming a hunk of meat. I asked her if she wanted to take a walk.

'In the mud and mire?' she asked. 'Sure.'

We followed a muddy, well-lit path, and as she nearly

slipped a time or two, I grabbed her hand and we walked like that. Her sarcasm softened into curiosity as we held hands. She asked me about my life back in the States; she shared with me "mad stories", from her travels to Austin, Texas to see a sister-in-law.

Her dress illuminated the dark and rapt by that ivory gleam, I wanted to have her all for me. I resisted the urge to ask about her man, the footballer in the newspaper clipping that my cousin had showed me, until she quizzed me on being single. 'I have someone at home but it's at the end of its line,' I said. Then I mentioned her footballer. My cousin was right. Off again, on again. I asked about the stalking. He wasn't stalking her, per se. 'He's in a job that allows him to stalk without stalking.' I wanted to ask more but I realised it wasn't important; I was flying home the next day. Her soft shoulders were gorgeous. She was so gorgeous. Naturally gorgeous. Whatever this was, it was tonight alone.

We rested on smooth boulders near an empty playground where she lit herself a cigarette, kicked off her ivory heels, wiggled her toes underneath the flesh-coloured stockings. Gazing at her pretty feet, I kidded her that in the States, only elderly women wear flesh-coloured stockings. 'That so?' she said. 'Well I've some decidedly un-old lady stockings at home.'

'Next to the old school uniform that doesn't fit?'

'Oh you'll eat those words. She *fit*s me, Yank.' She tossed her cigarette into the wet dirt and lifted her stray shoe and banged it against the cigarette, extinguishing it like she was crushing an insect. Then she dropped the shoe like it was a nuisance.

When she sat back, we kissed. She let her tongue twirl over mine and she sucked my tongue hungrily and then drew back from me, slowly, and closed her eyes, squeezed my hand. I tucked my hand around her waist and kissed her neck, dotting her long neck with affectionate kisses while her hand pried underneath my jacket, slipping under the front of my belt. The dance of her cold fingers on my skin made me wince.

I traced my tongue across her breast to the shiny satin material that hugged her breasts. I felt heat simmering on her cheeks, and my breathing was so hot and laboured that I lost my balance. She assisted me by grabbing my arms. 'I used to come here after church on Sundays,' she said, lowering her long right foot down onto the mud until it made a squishing noise. Then she stared at me like she was waiting to be scolded for muddying her feet but I approved so much of the peculiar gesture that I kissed her, harder and longer than before. Then she slipped her soiled foot back into her shoe and stabbed her heels into the mud until it made a pocking noise that turned me on. 'I used to come here and get what-for for dirtying my Sunday best digging for worms. Did you have a Sunday best that you got dirty?'

I described a horrible pale-blue pin-striped suit which I'd worn for my confirmation. 'But I was a good boy, I never got it dirty.' She liked that. She yanked off my belt and unzipped me. Then she held me and stared at my cock long and carefully in the dark.

'You don't feel to me like a good boy.' I shuddered. She crouched, somehow able to balance on her heels and she sucked my cock, bobbing her tongue along my shaft like she was sampling an ice cream flavour. She ran her forefinger in circles round to the top of my cock before taking me so fully into her mouth that I could feel her muffled breathing on me, her firm tongue so wet and so tender that before I could even fix my spot on the rocks I came, coming in a thick rush on her tongue, a coming that sent me reeling forward, my hand pressed into hard rock over her head as she slurped and lapped the last of me. When I was spent, she straightened herself and pointed down, to the very edge of her dress, just barely visible. 'You spilled on my – uniform. No worries,' she said, climbing down off the rocks and reaching back for me to take her hand, 'Ivory on ivory could hardly be called a stain.'

Gerri shared a flat with a girl who was away for the summer, leaving her the run of the place, including a backyard deck that overlooked a garden. Even in the dark and drizzle I could see white roses near a hedgerow.

Her heels pattered on the deck's wood, tapping out, in my mind, the syncopation of a passionate thumping – the two of us, I imagined, fucking out here in the "mistral", the faint rain cooling our hot skin. She seemed to know what I was thinking, and I drank the beer she gave me in one gulp. When she suggested she'd go inside and change and I insisted she stay in the bridesmaid dress.

'Well then,' she said, standing, swigging down the last of her beer, unhooking the skirt, 'this dress may not be a *uniform* but it weighs a ton.' The skirt part of the dress detached easily from the midriff and the much shorter hemline of her camisole generously showed off her legs. I let her wear my jacket and she stroked the lapels with exaggerated appreciation for the stitching. The backyard breezes were so cool and damp that the fresh air cleared away my beer and champagne buzz.

'I'm still fecking cold,' she said huddling under my jacket. Then she sat down squarely on my lap, and we kissed – kissing in no small part to keep warm – and we groped and clawed each other like teenagers. She grabbed my hand and put it under her camisole. 'Cold and *soaked*,' she said, half-closing her eye, as she let my fingers pry aside her panties.

The tips of my fingers grazed her pubic hair, then down sank tenderly into her wet sex. '*Soaked soaked soaked*,' she whispered into my ear. Her tongue plunged into my ear and the noise of it sounded like waves crashing.

I fingered her sex as she shifted here and there on my lap. She spread her long legs and leaned backwards as I supported her with my free arm, supporting her but also tickling and teasing her between her long legs until she grinned widely and bit down on her thin bright red lower lip. I kept up a sweet stroking rhythm, pausing now and then to tease her before pressing my finger up and down on her clit. When she opened her eyes to take in my stares, I studied her shimmering pupils – multiple shades of hazel, or maybe green – her greenish eyes gleaming in the pale light from her building's back door. In fact her eyes seemed to sparkle and to glint with each precise up-and-down flick of my fingers.

Feeling bolder, she bit my chin; I licked her nose; reaching behind, I unhooked the top of the dress, and lay it on the deck table. I lathered her breasts with voracious licks and nibbling. Then I slipped my finger fully inside her and held it. 'That's one safely harboured finger,' she said, biting my chin again, and biting down on her lower lip. She crossed her legs and squeezed my finger and when I withdrew my hands from between her legs I could feel how wet and slick she was. She was so heated and trembly that I had to help her stand up. 'Up,' I insisted, my cock so hard that even I had a hard time getting out of the chair.

'Demanding Yank you are,' she said. Though she was playing coy, her imagination was well ahead of me: she slipped off her panties and tossed them at me. Her soles were muddied. She peered back over her lovely shoulders at me and she slipped her feet back into her heels.

'Bend over,' I said 'Bend over. For me.'

She grinned. 'I'll do it as much for myself as for you,' she said.

Then she bent all the way down, grabbing her ankles. Her camisole slid down her hips and backside, a little avalanche of rippling silk, revealing all of her white ass which seemed to bask in its own light. She was giggling. Between her legs I saw her reddened face, upside down. Her hair dangled so low it almost touched the deck floor.

'Nimble, nimble woman,' I said.

'Yank, are you going to just stare at me and let me freeze?'

'I don't think there's a chance of you freezing,' I quipped, rushing to slip out of my pants and my underpants. My cock was so stiff and awkward that I had to hold it steady, press it in my palm, *grip* it, as if to confirm this pulsing sex were my own. It was hers as much as it was mine, I thought, and I stepped up to her and flicked my fingers between her legs, stroking up and down her thighs, pinching her ass skin playfully. Then I took a hard possessive hold of her hips and slipped myself between her cheeks – and in.

Our collective groan as our fleshy fires mingled must have woken up neighbours because dogs began barking. Fixed in place, we fell into a loving back and forth rhythm so sweet that I craned my neck and looked up at the cloudy sky, studying the moon that glowed behind those clouds, locating myself on the planet – the countryside, Ireland, night time – pulsing and grinding and moving myself in and out with Gerri whose tender cries were like a whispered song.

She had let go of her ankles and lifted herself halfway up to gain better balance, and as I closed my eyes I could feel from how tightly her pussy clenched my cock and the pitch of her cries that it was only a matter of moments before we'd rupture and come, and so I thrust harder and slower, encouraged by her long fingers that stroked my hip, and almost as I thought that we could go all night like this, I erupted, erupting as she bucked so hard against me that I nearly slipped on the deck floor, our moans now so loud and fierce that the dogs' barking intensified, and the barking drowned out even our laboured breathing as we collapsed onto the wet deck floor, clasping each other into a hot and necessary embrace.

I woke wrapped in quilts, in a bed. *Her* bed. The room was dark, snug. Outside a half opened door, I heard rummaging and turned on the lamp. On the mantle across from the bed I saw a framed photo of that footballer – the same one my cousin had shown me at the wedding. He was in that same rugby uniform. In fact, it was the same photo. Same guy.

Gerri strolled in, naked, sleepy-eyed, scheming. She tossed clothes on the bed with a kind of light-hearted spitefulness, as if we were newlyweds and I'd left my dirty clothes in the bathroom. But they weren't my clothes.

Girly leather shoes, blue, with flat heels and cute gold buckles were hooked on her fingers, dangling. 'These are the *pommes*,' she said, raising the pair into the air. '*Uniform*,' she enunciated, thrusting her hands at the clothes on the bed like they were a pile of autumn leaves. 'She – its – me.'

There was a blue plaid skirt and a grey shirt and a navy blue blazer. She put her hand into one leg of her dark blue tights. 'Even these fit.'

'That's no bridesmaid dress,' I said sitting up in bed.

She'd fixed drinks for us – sherry, from the wedding banquet – and as I lay there toasty and cared for in her room, she sat on the edge of the bed, naked, beaming, and we clinked glasses and toasted the night we'd made of it, kissing slowly between sips of the delicious sherry.

'Is he *the* guy?' I pointed to the mantle.

'That's himself. We're on again, off. Likely off, for good. I haven't taken the thing down because ...' Her voice trailed off.

'Professional footballer?'

'Somewhat so,' she said. 'He's a day job as well these days.'

I added that she wasn't the only one in the world with complicated relationships and she appreciated that.

'Now,' I said taking her sherry glass, 'let's see, does that uniform fit like you claim?'

She put her hands over her face and, laughing into her hands, she said she couldn't believe she'd even brought this subject up.

She made me leave the room while she changed. I fished a can of beer from her messy fridge. I threw my pants and shirt back on. I felt like I was being cast as a teacher to her schoolgirl but I preferred to think of myself as just what I was – a lucky fucker who had hooked up with a wonderful woman at a faraway wedding, a woman who happened to be having a newfound infatuation with her prim school duds. She seemed to take forever in there; I noticed her bridesmaid dress hanging near a closet and seeing it made me smile. I recalled the church earlier in the day, our banter behind the bandstand, our session out near the playground, her foot in the mud. I heard a whistle from the bedroom and I took that as my cue.

'You're right,' I said. 'This Yank has to eat his words.'

She had one hand rested on the dresser, the uniform skirt now so high above her knees it'd qualify as a *micro-mini* skirt. Her grey blouse was not tucked in and its tight sleeves were sloppily rolled over her elbows. Were she still in school, I told her, this get-up would get her in major trouble with the authorities.

She loved how she looked and it turned me on that she so adored herself. She bent her left leg for emphasis. She turned and pivoted and the sheer blue fabric that sheathed about her thighs were almost invisible as her fair skin glowed beneath it.

I let her know that were she still in school she'd get expelled for wearing this, because her legs were so long and so shapely and so erotic in those tight blue tights that any schoolboy with half a pulse would be so distracted he'd flunk all his exams. 'Even the girls would be driven to distraction,' I said.

'My English teacher had a terrible crush on me in my final term,' she said, putting on her blazer as if she were fixing to head off to his classroom right now.

I clasped her hips and kissed her. 'Pretty astonishing, nine years on,' I said.

'And what about the *pommes*?' She raised a foot and I studied the shoes' shiny buckles as she shuffled her feet back and forth on the carpeting.

She wanted me to strip her one item at a time. So I did. I removed each shoe, pausing to kiss her, running my hand up her back, tracing my forefinger along her cheek and her brow, unfastening her uniform's tie, unbuttoning the grey shirt as she shut her eyes, biting her lip as if recalling a schoolgirl fantasy – fucking her English teacher on his desk – or maybe seducing one of what must have been her countless admirers – and when I reached to undo her skirt she stopped me. 'Skirt stays on,' she said. I complied gladly.

As we kissed I lifted her up on to the dresser and she straddled me with her blue legs. I tore her bra off and cupped her breasts. I felt like I knew every inch of her skin and I knew her responses too – as if we'd been lovers for years rather than hours. I suckled on her nipples and her legs banged at me from behind, signalling for me to get on top. 'We are going to *fuck*,' she said. 'That we are,' I said, f-u-c-k.'

She grinned and I tried to pull down her tights but she stopped my hand, held my wrist still as she reached for her keys. Picking the sharpest key of the bunch, she smiled, aiming the key between her legs. 'Tear a hole,' she told me. I worked the key into the fabric, trying for a neat circle and as I worked she prodded and teased my crotch, 'C'mon, let her rip, it's for a good cause, Yank.'

I sliced the bevelled key into the fabric, carefully to keep the tights away from her skin and the tearing noise made my cock throb.

The keys splashed against the dresser and I was on her and inside her, my cock feeling the scratchy slit of her tights just before I felt her wet sex and the double – a scratch followed by a sweetness – quickened my pulse as we fucked, her legs locked behind me, her long arms splayed on the dresser, her eyes closed and our bodies virtually levitating against the hard wood surface – up and down and up – objects falling off the dresser like we'd raised an earthquake, an earthquake that rumbled until we both shivered, shivered and came, kissing madly with a satisfied perfection that left us both empty and full.

Somebody was knocking at her front door. Gerri got out of bed, naked save those tights and the torn fabric between her legs looked almost obscene. She wrapped herself in my jacket and went to the door. It was almost morning, I could tell from the bluish light around her bedroom window, I peeked outside and saw a police car. Objects lay strewn on the carpeting around the dresser. Those helpful keys. Her cute pommes with the leather buckle. A mess of hairpins.

From the foyer I heard her arguing. 'This is getting enough already.'

A man's voice protested, saying he'd seen the backyard light was on. 'And I'd reckoned you were staying at the wedding inn so I thought something might be up – is that so bad of me?'

I peered out the bedroom door and caught sight of a policeman, complete with yellow-green reflective vest and a large black cap. He was staring over Gerri's shoulder at me. I recognised him as the footballer on her mantle and I thought for a moment I was in some bizarre dream. His expression grew defensive and defeated as he saw me and their conversation ended abruptly. The door slammed and Gerri sighed as she came back into the bedroom, letting the robe crumple at her feet. I lay curled in bed as she had left me and I asked if everything was OK.

'Does *your* ex or whoever is in and out of your life these days knock on your door now and then?'

I said she didn't. 'But I sometimes knock on hers.'

She smiled. 'That's *him*.' She pulled back the curtains as the officer climbed back into his car, looking defeated and a little pathetic in his black and white uniform and patent leather shoes.

'Long way from the glory days on the rugby field,' I said.

'Oh, he still plays the footie,' she said, sighing. 'Can't live with, can't live ... you know the drill.' I said I did, and we lay in bed, our bodies pressed together and heard her man drive away.

I told her how much I loved this sensation of her legs against mine, and the sight of that tear in her tights when she'd gotten up from bed.

'Imagine I'd flashed him.'

'He might have arrested you for defacing a state issued school uniform.'

She giggled and we lay like that, and as our bodies stirred awake, we made love almost without moving, a long languorous hour on her bed, shifting, sliding, easing in and out, rising and falling on the sheets, she in me, me in her, sideways, gasping and groaning and swimming toward our pleasures, letting our limbs catch fire, slowly and searingly, as the sun rose and filled her room with a kind of streaming hot Irish light I won't soon forget.

Gerri and I didn't make a drama on my leaving and we decided to not exchange contacts. She helped me into my coat and patted me and we exchanged a final mutually satisfied gaze.

My cousin was waiting outside her place. He kidded me and wondered how I could walk after a night like that and as we drove the winding roads and long hours south to the airport the whole night replayed in my head so often that by the time we got to the airport the whole tryst felt like a dream.

At the security gate a beefy woman in a pale blue uniform and black polyester vest patted down my coat. 'No bridesmaid *she*,' my cousin quipped.

The officer felt something in the outside pocket of my jacket and asked me to remove it. 'What have you in there?'

I had no idea what it was and this seemed to irritate the officer who shot me a steely impatient glare.

It was her shoe. The pomme. The officer raised her brows and sighed. 'Your daughter's?' she said, sceptical and irritated.

'Not quite,' my cousin said, chuckling.

Inside the shoe was the pair of navy blue tights. The officer insisted I unroll 'what was inside', and as I did so, I couldn't tell whether she noticed that they were a pair of woman's tights torn at the crotch. My cousin whistled; I realised Gerri had shoved them into my pocket. I could hear her laughing all the way from Killybegs.

The officer asked me whether I wanted to 'secure my souvenir' into my carry-on bag and then they waited – the officer and my cousin – waiting with barely repressed grins as I did just that.

Uniform
by Rachel Charman

HEART POUNDING I WAITED for him. Alone in my uniform, this outer male shell, I felt my most suppressed self flooding out. I felt the ability to command with complete authority whatever I wanted. I opened my mouth and spoke aloud to try it. 'Lie down on the bed,' I barked. My voice had taken on a new quality; it was gruff, nonchalant, rumbling with a depth I hadn't heard in a woman's voice before.

I had bought the uniform via mail order from an army surplus company. I had chosen the ultimate masculine attire. I wanted something that would symbolise strength, force and authority. Then I wanted to take those things and twist them around myself like a garland. The day I ordered it over the phone, standing in my bedroom, measuring my waist, I felt stupid. Now, got up like a soldier boy and sneering in the mirror, I didn't feel stupid at all. I was simmering with desire.

Ever since I can remember I had been fascinated by men. As a child I mimicked the beautiful movement of boys, their spiking speech patterns, and their rough games. My mother despaired of me, but she needn't have worried. Just as I aped the boys that galloped around our neighbourhood in packs, I delighted in them. From a young age I adored their slim, straight shapes, almost envying them, but not quite. As we grew and the shape of my own body began to diverge from theirs, I began to appreciate the delicious difference. By my late teens I hungered for their long limbs and smooth, flat chests against mine.

It wasn't until I met him that the concept of two men began to excite me. I had been sitting with friends in a quirky city café one evening when he took to the shady stage, violin in one hand, a magical lightness of touch in the other. He began to play and every brimming note, every wail and murmur from his bow entangled me further. He was pale-skinned under the harsh coloured stage lights, always looking down at the floor as he played, lost in his own sound, his eyes shaded by thick, hay-coloured hair. He was a pinpoint in the dark room, a thin flame of light that promised electrifying heat. I stared long after my friends had left, waiting. Finally he looked at me and smiled, and I was his.

From there, he loped gracefully into my life, soft, slim and boyish, his bird-like frame balancing upright somehow as he seemed to be blown by a vector through life. He was doe-eyed and his hair was as soft and fine as my own. I couldn't look at him without imagining the dramatic arches of his ribs, the electric juts of his hips, and the delicate strength of his tapered fingers. He spoke rarely and softly, but always with gravity and absolute confidence. He was completely centred, grounded and resolute, which was the only way a man so fragile-looking could survive, particularly one so poor. He was like a wreath of exquisite paper flowers wrapped around a cast iron frame. I worshipped him.

I adored him because he wasn't like the other men I had been with. He seemed finer and more precious, and made even the trimmest of men look like hulking monsters. His limbs seemed as though they were made of light. It was out of that awestruck love that I began to imagine him alone, his hands running over his milk-white body, and then, two of him, or him and another man who would accentuate his gorgeous delicacy. Once the image found me it refused to leave.

We lay one night after making love when we first spoke of it. I was telling him about my tomboy childhood, and how I had always enjoyed playing the boy. I didn't want to be male, but there was something deeply exciting about taking the outer trappings of masculinity and wearing them about my round, feminine face. I wanted to play. He listened quietly in the way that he did, and then nodded, slowly, a smile breaking out across his face like a coil of incense smoke.

A few days later, I bought the uniform.

Standing alone, waiting for him in his crumbling, one-room flat, I looked again in the mirror and caught my breath. I had walked up and down the room in the dim light from the dusty bare light bulb, hands pocketed, ruffling my hair under the cap, practising a swagger. Then I returned to the cracked mirror on the wall. I was unable to resist touching the rough, hot, stiff khaki that encased me, restricting and yet emphasising the femininity of my body. My dim reflection was a threefold thing. It was female on first glance, as I recognised my familiar features; then it was male, as the peaked officer's cap drew out my cheekbones and the clothes lengthened my limbs; then, it was female again, the straight cut of the jacket wrapped tight around my chest and hips. I shifted in my polished parade shoes and felt again the hard cock warming against my thigh, and my throat dried. I ran my hands over my hips, feeling the leather straps that held my cock bite playfully into my skin.

Suddenly I heard the door rattle and I spun round, breaking my narcissistic gaze to see him step lightly into the flat. He shut the warped door quietly, and then simply stood, looking at me. I waited for a moment, keeping my face neutral as my mind raced. I felt the stiff shirt collar around my throat and caught the gleam of the buttons of my jacket, and something instinctive kicked in. As if the clothes I wore took over, I strode across the room to my lover and paused, my hands in my pockets, just inches from his lips.

He was tall but so was I, and standing like this, we were eye to eye. I appeared relaxed, with my feet wide apart and a smile on my face. It wasn't my own smile, but one I had seen on the faces of hundreds of men throughout my life. It was the smug, cocky grin of a man enjoying taking his time. My man stood with his hands at his sides, his eyes flickering. I placed a fingertip at his mouth, and traced it down, over the rough slope of his jaw, down the jumping line of his throat, his chest, his belly, and then lightly, as if not at all, held my fingertips at his belt.

'Like it?' I growled, still grinning in that strange way. Still he didn't move, but nodded, his eyelids hovering over wide irises. Slowly I began to circle with my fingers, keeping our bodies apart by a hair's breadth, but just enough to sweetly torment us both. I kissed him and his lips found mine hungrily. With some effort I tore myself away from him and ordered him to undress.

He removed his clothes smoothly, slowly, as if he was alone, but I could see his desire even as he did so. I heard the catch in his breath and felt the tension thick in the air, like smoke. He lay on his cramped bed, stretched out like a feast for me and me alone.

I sat on the edge of the bed and looked at him. The fair, fine hair on his skin rose eagerly, seeming to follow my gaze as it roved over him. I kissed him again, and then broke away as he reached to embrace me. I pushed his hands to his sides firmly and looked at him again, my heart swelling at the leonine muscles of his stomach and the graceful lines of his shoulders. He was hard and I knew he ached for me to kneel down and take him in my mouth as I had done so many times before, but I wouldn't. As I waited, my hand occasionally dancing over his waif-like frame, his hand crept tentatively to his cock, but I brushed it away. He would have to wait for that.

Moving quickly now, I turned him over and was

momentarily taken in by his beauty from a different angle. I regained myself hurriedly and stood up. I undid the buckle on my belt and unfastened my trousers, freeing my cock. I held it against myself for a moment as I lavished kisses along his spine, and then gently pushed it into him.

He gasped and for a few seconds we were still, paralysed by the sudden pleasure. I laid along his back, my hands over his either side of his head, and together we moved, my hips rolling slowly back and forth as he rose to meet my movements. I felt the warmth of his skin through my jacket and shirt as my breasts pressed through the harsh fabric. My cock pressed hard against me with each delicious stroke and I felt myself growing wetter. Beneath us the tattered camp bed creaked and I listened out of habit for the rats scuttling inside the wall cavities. Then he groaned and I was drawn back to him as he writhed, flourished and glowed in the midst of all this dirty and decaying poverty. I dug my hands into this thick, pale hair and pushed harder and faster, feeling inside the familiar melting and sliding sensation at the base of my belly.

Gradually I felt his need for me grow. His hands chafed against the rough woollen blanket, missing my skin. He turned his head now and then to glance at me, and at one point, his eyes almost seemed to plead. When I could bear it no longer I pulled back, breathless, inflamed but not yet satisfied.

He turned on the narrow bed and reached for me with that strange agility and lightness that always left me unnerved and in awe of him. Within a few moments he had stripped me of my parade shoes and stiff khaki trousers, as well as my harness and cock. He whipped my tie from around my neck and yanked open my shirt and jacket, before burying his face in my neck, his hands racing over my breasts and stomach. Only now did I give in to him, arching my spine and tilting my head back. My cap fell from my head as he lifted me onto his lap and we lay down, locked at the mouth.

I had been so lost at the feel of his mouth on mine and of his hands dancing on my skin that when he pressed into me, slow and hard, I cried out at the sudden pleasure. I rolled into his stroke, driving him deeper, and he gave a sort of sob. Now we were both frantic, our hips jerking, our hands clawing at each other, at ourselves, at the blankets and the walls. I knelt up and held myself above him, still in my open shirt and jacket. He was glorious, his eyes closed and every muscle and nerve tensed. Our orgasm, as it gripped us and tore the breath from our lungs, was a cacophony of sensation and sentiment. I felt him filling me from inside, I felt his hips against my thighs, his hands on my breasts, and my hands pressed against the cold, damp walls.

I felt my borrowed masculinity tumbling around me, like ribbons, like confetti, as my femininity burst through in flesh and tears and sighs and half-whispered words. I felt the liberation he gave me, with his sensual fucking and his ambiguous desires and his soft nature, to delight in the man and the woman in me at the same time.

This Woman is Dangerous
by Landon Dixon

FRANK DRURY STARED OUT at the black ribbon of road from his hiding place behind the billboard. But his thoughts weren't on his duties as a California Highway patrolman, monitoring the Pacific Coast Highway for late-night speeders.

He was thinking of that picture-poster all the boys had kept in their lockers during the war – the pin-up of Betty Grable from the backside, hands on her hips, peeking over her shoulder with a come-hither look, clad in a swimsuit that showed off her fine, rounded bottom and million-dollar legs. And he gripped his hard cock in the warm, worn leather of his motorcycle glove and stroked, sitting astride his police Harley-Davidson.

It'd been a tough year for Frank after the war. He'd come home to find that his wife had run off with his best friend, sold off all of his belongings. The home fires had been squelched long ago for this returning GI. So, he'd drifted. Before finally mustering out of one uniform and into another.

Now he wore the black horsehide leather jacket, tan whipcord breeches and tall leather boots, the peaked cap and Sam Browne belt, of a motorcycle cop. But just like in the Army, his mind wandered. In this case, onto Betty and those gorgeous gams of hers, that ripe, delicious ass, as he stroked strong and sure up and down the long, throbbing length of his cock.

There was hardly any traffic, anyway. It was a cool, cloudy night, a Wednesday, the only bulletin to come over the radio about some lunatic who had escaped from the Agnews Insane Asylum 20 miles east in Santa Clara. White female, age 26, black on blue, 5'6" tall, 120 pounds; convicted of jealously killing a man when she'd found him back in the arms of his loving wife, spared the death penalty pending a long, peaceful stay at the asylum. 'This woman is considered dangerous', the dispatcher had concluded.

But Frank wasn't concerned. They'd probably find the dame squirrelled up a tree not far from the nuthouse. The big, curly-haired galoot grinned, stars in his big, brown eyes, hand shifting into fourth on his cock, riding it hard, balls against the warm leather seat tingling.

A car shot by on the highway. Frank blinked, cursed. He tucked his hard-on back into his pants and kick-started his motorcycle. You just couldn't ignore a car doing 80 – with no lights on. The motorcycle roared to life, and the engine throbbed a fat, wet chorus between Frank's muscular legs.

He rolled out onto the road and gunned it, zooming after the speeding shadow, all his lights on and siren wailing. And he easily caught up to the darkened car on a curve, signalled with a gloved hand for the driver to pull over.

She did, finally turning on her own lights when Frank skidded to a stop in front of the car, on the gravel shoulder of the road. He was briefly spotlighted in her high beams, unable to see, the vehicle's powerful engine racing.

He strode out onto the road and over to the driver-side door of the car. 'What's the big idea, speeding with no lights on? You trying to kill yourself!?'

It was a Buick super convertible, black as the night, polished like the stars. And the woman behind the wheel was even more stunning: a slim, sleek figure dressed entirely in white – a nurse's uniform – blonde hair haloing her head, a perfect oval face smooth as a cameo, large blue eyes and lush red lips. Her arms were bare in the crisp uniform, slender and lithe, like her legs, which flowed out of her short skirt in shiny white stockings.

'I'm sorry, officer,' she pouted, glowing in the beam of Frank's flashlight. 'I was just in a hurry, I guess, not thinking about what I was doing.'

'Uh-huh.' Frank stared at her breasts, taut mounds wrapped tight by her uniform. The nametag above her left breast read: Nurse Nancy Tate. 'You work in a hospital?'

She looked up into the light. 'A kind of hospital – the Agnews Insane Asylum.'

Frank's gloved hand caressed the butt of his gun. He licked his lips. 'Yeah? I hear one of your patients escaped tonight.'

The woman smiled coyly. 'Yes, she did.'

Frank cleared his throat, gruffly said, 'Wasn't you, huh?' The height and weight measurements looked close, and a quick dye job could've taken care of the hair.

She laughed, like the tinkling of bells. 'Sometimes it feels like it – when I finally get off. But this is my car, Officer ...?'

'Frank Drury.'

'Frank. And I've got my identification in my purse, if you would like to see it.'

Frank shone his beam onto the steering column, bent his head down to read the registration. And sweet jasmine flooded his senses, as Nancy squirmed slightly in her seat, the living, breathing, pulsing picture of femininity, her warm body so very close. It'd been a long time between women for Frank, too long.

The registration read: Nancy Tate, 1245 Season Street, Palo Alto. 'Well, you were speeding, with no lights on?' he rasped, lifting his head, the blood rushing back making him dizzy.

'I'm sorry, Frank. I've been so awfully absentminded since my husband died a year ago.' Her eyes dropped, her hands rubbing the hem of her skirt on her stockinged thighs.

'It's terrible not having a man around. A woman gets so ... lonely.' She looked up again. 'Are you married, Frank?'

He grunted. 'Not anymore.'

Then he jumped, almost dropped the flashlight. As he felt Nancy's hand grip his cock, still rigidly outlined against the front of his uniform pants. 'Then you know how it is,' she breathed, her hand warm and soft, her stroke soothingly erotic. Frank instantly hardened the last couple of inches he'd lost when he'd rolled out.

'And I really don't think my insurance company could handle another speeding ticket,' the woman purred, gently, tantalisingly rubbing Frank's pulsating cock through his pants.

She looked so clean and pure in her nurse's uniform. But Frank knew that nurses knew their way around a man's body. That was something else he'd learned in the Army.

'Is there someplace we can go ... to discuss this further, Frank? I haven't enjoyed the company of a man in such a looong time.'

Frank stared down at Nancy's stroking hand on his uniformed cock, flooding his body with a deliciously tingling heat. The flashlight beam wavered, and he growled, 'Follow me!'

He led the way off the highway and up a steep dirt road that led to the top of a bluff overlooking the ocean. And his palms went even damper in his gloves, his cock surging, when he saw her fall in behind in her car.

He parked his motorcycle 30 feet from the edge of the cliff, and she pulled up alongside. Then he was off his bike, she out of her car, and they were in each other's arms, kissing fiercely like they'd been far apart for far too long a time.

Frank crushed the woman's lithe, white-clad body against his, Nancy clutching the smooth, supple leather of Frank's jacket, their mouths working, devouring one another's lips. The surf gently creamed against the rocks far down below, the moon sliding out from behind the clouds to paint the ocean silver.

They swirled their tongues together, Frank cupping Nancy's face in his hands, as she slipped her own hands in under his jacket and around his waist, briefly jostling his gun in its holster. He quickly pushed her up against the side of the car and grasped her firm, warm breasts through her uniform, groped them. She tilted her head back and moaned, and he sunk his teeth into the silky, perfumed skin of her neck.

There was no time to undress, their pent-up need too great. He roughly squeezed her tits and urgently sucked on her nipples through the thin cloth of her uniform, wetting the material, pulling on her hardened buds, biting into them. She grabbed on to his cock again and pumped it, feeling the ardent pulsing of the man through his breeches.

'Fuck me, Frank!' she cried. 'I need you to fuck me – now!'

He pulled her around to the rear of the car, lifted her light as a feather up onto the trunk. She eagerly pulled her short, white skirt up and parted her white stockinged legs, revealing her black-furred pussy.

Frank hesitated, but only for a moment. The questions could come later. Right now, he needed answers – to his burning want. He unbuttoned his fly and drew out his cock, plunged it into Nancy's wet, welcoming pussy.

'Yes!' they groaned, truly home again.

He gripped her silken legs to his leathered chest and rocked her back and forth on the gleaming metal with his thrusting cock. Her brilliant white body in the moon and starlight dazzled his eyes, her oven-hot pussy sucking on his pistoning dong, making his balls boil.

She gripped her tits and moaned, rolling her head from side to side, taking Frank's pumping cock full-length over and over, harder and faster. His leather jacket squeaking, gun jumping, the huge, looming man violently filling her need, slamming her shimmering into a sea of sensation.

They were headed over the edge.

'No! Not yet!' Nancy suddenly cried, scrambling up onto her elbows. 'Fuck me in the ass, Frank! I want you to fuck me in the ass!'

He kept on churning her cunt, her frantic words not fully registering. And when they did, it was all he could do to keep from exploding inside her.

She climbed down off the trunk, back onto her feet. Then she turned around and bent over and splayed her hands out on the black metal, thrust her bare bum out from under her rolled-up skirt, legs slightly parted.

Frank had done a lot in his 25 years, but never that before. 'You want me to–'

'I'm dirty, Frank! Fuck my ass! Please!'

She grabbed onto his already pussy-slick cock and pulled it against her cunt lips, slathering it even more with her wetness. Then she fitted the shining, mushroomed cap into her butt cleft, as he pulled her taut cheeks apart. She pushed back, he forward, penetrating her ass, sliding into her anus.

It was hotter and tighter than any woman's pussy, and he grunted, 'Jesus!' Nancy quivering on the end of his buried cock.

He slid his hands up onto her waist and dug his fingers in, pumping his hips, fucking her bum. Her buttocks shivered and legs trembled, nails scraping on metal, as he relentlessly drove her ass.

She dove a hand down in between her legs and desperately rubbed her pussy, screaming, 'God in heaven! I'm coming!' She shook out-of-control, vibrating wildly with orgasm, the man's ploughing cock filling her to bursting with wicked pleasure.

It was too much for Frank. He recklessly reamed her chute and then jerked, bucked, spraying searing semen into

Nancy's anus. His shield flashed and his peaked cap tumbled off his head, as he emptied himself into the shrieking woman.

Only when he heard the banging on the trunk of the car, did he stagger backwards, out of her. Because the banging was coming from *inside* the trunk. 'What-what have you got in there!?' he gasped.

Nancy smiled, shining white in front of him. And before his shattered reflexes could react, she'd pulled the flashlight out of his belt and slugged him alongside the head with it.

She held the semi-conscious man up like a good nurse, helped him in behind the wheel of her car. So that by the time he'd shaken off some of the cobwebs, he was already barrelling towards the edge of the cliff, his heavy, booted foot on the accelerator.

He grunted, heaved the wheel over to the left at the last moment. The car spun around in a half-circle, its rear wheels briefly skidding right over the side of the bluff, before finding traction on the grass again.

Frank gritted his teeth and pointed the car at Nancy running for the dirt road that led down to the highway. She was easy to see in her uniform, in the roaring car's headlights. He clipped her with the front bumper, sending her flying.

He opened the trunk of the car, helped the bound and gagged woman inside out into the cool night air.

'She was going to kill me!' the black-haired, blue-eyed, 5'6", 120 pound female wailed. 'Her name isn't Nancy Tate – it's Elizabeth Starr! She said I'd gotten off too easy killing her husband!'

Officer Frank Drury held the raving woman at arm's-length, staring at the stencilled black lettering on the breast of her blue pyjamas: Agnews Insane Asylum.

'She's crazy!' the woman screamed.

Splendide Girl
by Courtney James

I DIDN'T TAKE THE job because of the uniform, gorgeous though it was. That was just a bonus. I took it because Michael Benington was offering me the chance to make a long-held dream come true.

When I read in the local paper that Benington was planning to re-open the Splendide, I was determined to get a job there. The cinema, opened in the late 1920s, had once been the most impressive building in town. Its Art Deco interior was decorated in rich shades of gold and red, and its bar was fitted out with gleaming bronze rails. The auditorium boasted a huge crystal chandelier and two rows of love seats right at the back, where couples could sit together in cosy comfort to watch the film – or not, as they chose. At the interval, a Wurlitzer organ would rise up through a trapdoor in the stage, and the audience would be entertained with a selection of popular tunes. I was taken there a few times when I was a child, and even though the once-plush seats were rather moth-eaten and the owner could no longer afford to employ an organist, I still thought it was the most magical place on earth. When I grew up, I told myself, I would work in that glorious picture palace.

Then a new shopping mall appeared on the edge of town. Among its many attractions was an eight-screen multiplex cinema. Even though most of the screens weren't much larger than the average front room, the Splendide couldn't compete with the choice it offered, and within a year it had been forced to close. It reopened briefly as a bingo hall, but the town centre as a whole was in decline, shoppers lured away by the delights of the mall, and soon the Splendide was boarded up and forgotten.

Michael Benington was determined to change that. An avowed cinema buff who had made his money in property development, he announced his plan to buy and run the Splendide. He intended to restore it to the beauty of its pre-war heyday, and once it was complete, he would be actively recruiting staff.

I watched as the boards came down and the builders moved in. Benington worked fast, and three months later I was one of almost a hundred people who applied to work at the Splendide. I'd like to think my genuine love for the building and my knowledge of film helped me land the job. In truth, it had as much to do with the fact I fitted Benington's vision of what a Splendide usherette should look like. In keeping with the cinema's beginnings, he planned to screen classic black-and-white movies alongside current releases and the subtitled art house films the multiplex never showed. He really wanted the audience to feel they were stepping back in time as they entered the cinema's beautifully restored foyer. This meant proper uniforms for the staff, rather than the drab polo shirts and casual slacks more usual elsewhere.

Benington had a sample usherette's uniform draped over a mannequin by his desk. It consisted of a short, fitted red jacket with gold buttons down the front, a tight skirt that came to mid-thigh level and a perky pillbox hat. It was, he told me, designed to be worn with high heels and stockings, not tights. Impractical but sexy, particularly when you were as short and busty as I was. With my cloud of curly red hair peeking from beneath the hat, I knew I would look like a pocket dynamo from a Busby Berkeley musical. He clearly realised that, too. 'You have all the attributes I'm looking for, Kirsty,' he said, a wickedly curving smile on his face.

'The job's yours if you want it.'

I wanted it very much, and a week later I was slipping into my uniform for the first time, ready to begin work as a Splendide girl. The clothes seemed to demand appropriate underwear beneath them, so I'd treated myself to a black bra, French-cut satin knickers and deep suspender belt with six straps from a vintage lingerie shop. As I hooked my seamed black stockings to the suspenders, I felt like a 40s siren, my hourglass curves defined and emphasised by the flattering underwear. Pulling the jacket and skirt over the top made me strangely horny, as though I was surrendering to a lover's caress. Looking at my reflection in the bedroom mirror, I couldn't resist the urge to smooth my hands over my body, following the sleek lines of my breasts and hips. Even though I knew I ran the risk of being late on my first day on the job, I gave in to the overwhelming impulse to lift my skirt and touch myself through my knickers. My pussy seemed to blossom as I stroked it, growing hotter and wetter by the moment.

In my mind, I was standing on the stage at the Splendide, with an audience of anonymous voyeurs revelling in my performance. Even though I couldn't see their faces, I knew each one, male and female, was rapt with lust, turned on by the sight of my fingers snaking into my underwear and up into my cunt. The screen was dark, the only spotlight on me as I frigged myself to a swift, breathless climax. In reality, my knees sagged and I clutched on to the mirror as I came. Taking a moment to clean myself up, I was soon out of the house and on my way with a wiggle in my walk, looking forward more than ever to starting work at the Splendide.

The glamour of the job wore off more quickly than I might have expected. It was fun to show cinema-goers to their seats with the aid of a cute little torch, and when I stood at the front of the auditorium with my tray of peanuts and ice creams, I never failed to get admiring looks and even blatant come-ons from my customers. I simply hadn't realised how even the most skilfully plotted, stylishly shot film could become tedious once you'd seen it six times in a row. If the film was bad to begin with – and many of them were – by the end of its run I was left feeling that I would rather claw my own eyes out than watch it again.

Saturday night made up for the tedium to some extent. Michael had declared it to be "cult cinema night", with midnight screenings of films for a devoted and, in some cases, debauched fan base. *The Sound Of Music* was especially popular, with the audience singing along to the soundtrack dressed as nuns, Nazis and Julie Andrews. Most fun of all were *Rocky Horror Picture Show* nights. The Splendide would be packed with punters in fancy dress who knew all the responses to shout at the screen and when to throw confetti, squirt water pistols and generally cause mayhem in the aisles. It seemed half the men in the area had been waiting for this excuse to dress up in drag, prancing around in basques, stockings and tiny knickers that often struggled to contain their cocks.

Michael, who sat in one of these shows, was surprised at just how enjoyably raucous proceedings became. When someone dressed as an usherette came on stage to perform a seductive burlesque routine to the film's opening song, a light bulb must have gone off over his head. On the following Monday, he called all the girls who worked as usherettes to a meeting so he could share his idea with us. He thought it would add to the spirit of proceedings if we made a special modification to our uniform on *Rocky Horror* nights. Specifically, he wanted us to leave our skirts off. I expected at least one of the girls to object, but no one did. Perhaps the others knew, just as I did, how downright horny we would look in our tight jackets and little hats with our stocking tops and suspenders blatantly on display. We fitted in perfectly with the kinky mood of the film, and sold so many snacks every time we appeared in our underwear Michael – only half-jokingly, I thought – suggested we dress like that all the time.

Much as I enjoyed the cult classic nights, I knew I was going to have to find some way of keeping the boredom at bay on quiet afternoons at the Splendide. The germ of an idea was planted one Wednesday or Thursday when I was helping a man to his seat after the screening had begun. I passed the love seats, which Michael was promoting as a special feature of the cinema, with "champagne packages" that offered bottles of fizz for couples to enjoy as they watched the film. In the circle of light from my torch, I caught the briefest glimpse of a man's hand cupping his lover's bare breast as they kissed, oblivious to what was happening on the screen. It didn't surprise me that couples grew amorous in the Splendide – the decadent surroundings and seats made for two practically demanded it – but that glimpse of naked female flesh was so unexpected, so deliciously rude, it had my juices flowing. Much as I wanted to linger to see whether things would progress further, the door at the back of the auditorium had opened and another patron was looking for his seat. With a small sigh of disappointment, I went to assist him. By the time I managed to sneak back to the love seats to get another look at the couple in action, she was buttoned up demurely once more and their attention was fully on the film.

My voyeuristic curiosity had been piqued, and I started making regular circuits of the auditorium during screenings, to see whether I could spot more naughty goings-on. In the dim light from the emergency exit signs I spotted plenty to fuel my erotic yearnings. It wasn't just lusty, deep-throated kissing and groping through clothes, though I saw plenty of that. Girls would have unzipped their boyfriend's fly and were slowly stroking his cock, or the lad would have his hand up her skirt as he fingered her. On one memorable occasion, a couple had manoeuvred themselves in one of the love seats so she was sitting on his lap. They appeared to be wrapped up in the fluffy romantic comedy they were watching, but I could tell from the gentle way she was rocking back and forth that she was impaled on his cock and fucking him to a slow climax. The sight was enough to have me slipping out of the room, knowing there was a good 25 minutes before Jennifer Aniston finally realised she'd been in love with her best friend since the start of the film and the credits started rolling. I dashed into the ladies' and locked myself in a cubicle. Hitching up my uniform skirt and pulling down my knickers, I rubbed my clit frantically 'til I came.

I would have gone on like that for ever, getting the odd guilty thrill to ease me through the day, if Michael hadn't scheduled the screening of a highly controversial French film. Billed as the story of a doomed love affair, it was actually little more than a series of highly graphic sex scenes. These, the publicity claimed, were not simulated.

Predictably, it attracted people who wouldn't normally sit through a foreign language film but simply wanted to watch the lead actor and actress fucking. Watching it for the first time, I couldn't decide whether the sex was real or staged, but it was certainly getting me horny. It seemed to be having the same effect on the audience. Normally, the soundtrack of any film the Splendide showed would be punctuated with the sound of sweets being unwrapped, coughing, even the odd phone ringing, despite the on-screen request that all mobiles had to be switched off. Today, there were no extraneous noises, just a tense, excited silence.

Almost without being aware of what I was doing, I unbuttoned my uniform jacket halfway down. I tweaked my nipple through my bra, feeling the little bud stiffen immediately. My pussy, hot and liquid, demanded my attention, and I would have stuck a hand up my skirt to satisfy the itch if I hadn't heard a sudden noise.

I tried to place the strangely familiar, rhythmic slapping

sound. When I glanced round to see where it was coming from, I spotted a man sitting in the front row, a couple of feet from where I was standing. He had his cock in his hand and was wanking steadily. My mouth watered as I registered just how big it was. More than anything, I wanted to touch and taste it.

On feet that seemed to belong to someone else, I shuffled over to him. 'May I help you with that, sir?'

'What did you have in mind?' he asked.

There were empty seats to either side of him, and I dropped into one of them. I closed my fingers around his shaft. 'I figured you could use a hand with this,' I murmured. 'I saw how the film was turning you on.'

'Oh, it wasn't,' he said. 'I just have a thing about cute redheaded usherettes. Watching you with your uniform half-undone, playing with your tits, was hornier than anything in this pretentious, self-regarding movie.'

My hand shuttled up and down his cock. 'So, you like me in this uniform, do you?'

'Mmm,' he replied, 'but I'd like it even more if you lost the skirt. Just like you do on *Rocky Horror* nights.'

So he was a regular here. Was he one of the men who squeezed into women's underwear to watch the film, unashamedly pervy and in touch with his feminine side, or was he a strait-laced Brad, needing to be introduced to the joys of filthy sex? So many delicious possibilities ...

I glanced to my left, then my right. No one was paying us the slightest attention. As the couple on screen were currently having vigorous sex on a kitchen table, that was hardly surprising. 'Since you ask so nicely ...' I reached behind me and unzipped my skirt. Then I stood briefly, so I could shimmy out of it, marvelling again at how much sexier it felt to where half a uniform, rather than a full one.

'And the knickers,' he said. 'Beautiful as they are, I need to see you without them.'

He was asking me to do something incredibly risky, but

given he was already sitting with his cock out in the open I could hardly refuse. Not that I wanted to.

Knickerless, I dropped to my knees on the scratchy carpet and reached for his cock again. This time, I made an O of my red-painted lips and engulfed his helmet. He hissed through his teeth in pleasure as I swallowed more and more of him down. I was glad my pillbox hat was pinned securely in place, otherwise it would surely have fallen from my head as it bobbed vigorously in his lap. He must have been eating popcorn earlier, because I could taste the lingering traces of butter and salt he'd transferred from his palm as he wanked. It made me want to suck him until he came, but he whispered, 'Let me fuck you, pretty usherette.'

Obediently, I stopped what I was doing and climbed on to his lap, sitting so we were both facing the screen. I didn't believe I really needed the extra stimulation of watching the fictional couple have sex, but over the last few weeks I had come to the conclusion I was a born voyeur. With the subtitles conveying every last syllable of their dirty talk, I realised my lover was getting something out of the film, too, despite his earlier criticism. As the words 'Let me stick it up your arse' appeared in bold white type, I heard him give a lustful groan. That groan increased in volume as I slowly sank down on his cock, my pussy taking him in its tight, silken grip.

I bounced on his groin, loving the way his thick shaft filled me so exquisitely. He fumbled with the rest of my jacket buttons, undoing the garment completely. He kneaded my tits through my bra, his lips nuzzling my neck.

'God, that feels amazing,' I muttered. My hand dropped between my thighs, so I could roll my clit in small, tight circles. My vision was beginning to swim, the subtitles becoming a blur as my pleasure mounted. The dialogue on screen gave way to throaty grunts of uninhibited pleasure, echoing the noises we were making.

Beneath me, my lover's body stiffened and he came,

clutching hard at my tits as he did. Throwing my head back, I let my own orgasm consume me, burning through me like a flash fire and leaving me spent.

When I finally mustered the strength to slip off his lap, I murmured, 'That was so good, but I'd better get dressed. I don't want to be caught like this when the lights go up.'

'Think what amazing publicity it would be for the Splendide,' he replied. 'Come along and see the film that's so horny it makes the usherettes fuck total strangers.'

'But you're not going to be a stranger, are you?' I asked as I scrambled back into my skirt, aware that we hadn't even exchanged names. 'I am going to see you again, aren't I?'

'Of course.' His tone was seductive. 'Saturday night is *Rocky Horror* night, and I'll be here.'

'How will I recognise you?' I asked, thinking of all the weird and wonderful costumes the audience chose to wear.

'Oh, I'll be easy to spot.' His next words gave me the feeling my life was about to become very interesting. 'I'll be dressed as an usherette.'

Lower Learning
by Lynn Lake

I HELD CHRISTINE'S HAND and we walked up the flagstone steps to Dr Herges's home on campus. The school bell had just gone off, signalling the start of graduation ceremonies, and there was hardly anybody around outside.

We stopped at the red front door of the grey brick house, and I turned to Christine. 'Ready?'

She gulped, and nodded.

She looked so cute in her school uniform – white blouse, red plaid pleated skirt, white knee-high socks, and polished black shoes. Cute and sexy, what with the top three buttons of her blouse undone and the skirt hemmed higher than regulation on her thighs. I was dressed exactly the same.

I squeezed her hand, kissed her softly on her violet-painted lips, and rang the doorbell.

No answer.

I rang a second time.

And we heard footsteps coming down the hallway inside.

Christine turned to run. But I held on tight to her, our palms joined together by dampness.

Dr Herges flung the door open. He was dressed in his ceremonial black gown, black mortarboard atop his curly, salt and pepper hair, white and red fur collar around his shoulders. He was obviously late for the convocation.

'Yes, can I help you girls?' he said.

'Hi, Dr Herges!' I bubbled. 'Don't you remember us – Samantha Mulvane and Christine Miller?'

His clear, brown eyes narrowed. 'Samantha and Christine. You two were expelled over a year ago.' He glanced down at our uniforms, the school crest over the left breasts of our blouses. 'How did you get hold of those uniforms? You were supposed to turn all of yours in when you left.'

I tossed my long, red hair back, blinked my frank, blue eyes, noticing how the man briefly studied the exposed skin on our chests and thighs. 'We're sorry, Dr Herges,' I said. 'You know how much we loved school.'

'Loved getting into trouble, you mean. I had to discipline both of you countless times.'

I rubbed my bare bottom under my skirt, using Christine's held hand. 'We remember.' I looked at the black-haired girl and grinned. She looked back at me, her dark eyes shining, full red lips wet.

'Anyway, I'm late for convocation. So, if you girls wouldn't mind ...'

He stepped closer, to get by us. And I said, 'You like being spanked yourself, don't you, Dr Herges? At the Gentlemen's Club.'

He froze, his handsome, square-jawed face suddenly gone ashen.

'See, Christine and I worked there for a while, after you expelled us in our final year of school. And we saw you with ... Madame X. In the dungeon.' I fluttered my long eyelashes, wetted my own lips with the tip of my pink tongue. 'We know what it feels like to be spanked, Dr Herges; spanked good for being bad. And we can dish it out just as well as you used to give it to us – if you want.'

Christine's hand tightened in mine, her hard nipples straining the thin cotton of her top, like mine.

'Well, I really should ...' Dr Herges began, staring into Christine's gleaming eyes.

We slowly advanced on the man.

'There are a couple in the lower drawer there,' he said, his deep, rich voice breaking slightly.

Dr Herges was bent forward at the foot of his bed, gripping the brass railing. His ceremonial gown was up around his waist, his bare white legs slightly parted and pale rounded bum stuck out, cheeks quivering.

'Got 'em!' Christine yelped, pulling two straps out of the drawer.

She handed one to me, and we took up position on either side of the man; Christine on the right, because she's left-handed. The straps were foot-long, three-inch-wide, quarter-inch thick slabs of black, pebbled, flexible leather. We remembered them well from the sessions in Dr Herges' office in the Admin Building.

'Well, come on, girls!' he yelled, his face red. 'Spank me!'

We looked at each other. He was still trying to order us around, like we were still in school.

Christine and I placed the ends of the straps against Dr Herges' bare buttocks, making him jump. We gently rubbed his twitching flesh, teasing him, not yet giving him what he so desperately wanted, and wanted hard. We'd seen him get his bottom beaten to a berry-red pulp by Madame X, heard him scream for more. Penance, perhaps, for all of the brutal punishment he'd inflicted on countless boys and girls at the School.

Christine tapped his right cheek, I his left. The bed railing rattled. 'Please, girls!' he hissed.

'That's more like it,' I said, smiling at Christine. We slapped Dr Herges' ass together.

He groaned.

We slapped harder. He shivered.

We smacked his bum, the crack of hard leather against soft flesh echoing in the stuffy upstairs bedroom. Dr Herges stopped shaking and thrust out his butt even further to meet our blows.

Christine whacked his ass. I lifted the ugly old strap right over my head and whistled it down onto the man's bum, crashing it home. We beat Dr Herges' buttocks, whaling his unprotected flesh, colouring his skin, making him jump to the thunderous crack of our straps.

We stared at one another, our nostrils flared and mouths open, flushed faces shiny with perspiration, flailing Dr Herges' bum. We took out all of our recent frustrations and failures on the bent-over, hard-breathing man, rocking him with our rage, shocking his buttocks to a burning red mess with our brutal efforts.

He grunted and groaned, enjoying getting his ass pulverized, blistered so badly that our strap strokes flashed white on his brick-red skin, raising ridges of hardened flesh where they savagely landed. He'd never beaten any of us *this* hard, but Christine and I didn't let up, smashing the man's bum almost simultaneously, incessantly; our bodies shaking and nipples buzzing and pussies brimming with juices.

The heated straps sang through the crackling air, wickedly stinging Dr Herges' bottom over and over and over.

Until Christine suddenly dropped her strap, and I dropped mine, and we rushed into each other's arms, wildly kissing and frenching. Dr Herges didn't even notice for a while, his body still rhythmically jerking with imaginary blows, beaten beyond even the point of feeling. And when he did finally notice, it was too late.

I caught Christine's thrashing tongue between my teeth and sucked on it. She wriggled it free, bit into my puffy lower lip, drawing blood and drinking it. I spat in her face, and she slapped my face. We stared meaningfully into each other's glazed eyes; and turned our attention back to Dr Herges.

We each took an arm and led the shaken man over to the side of his bed, pushed him down on top of it. He winced when his ravaged bum made contact with the bedspread, then squirmed against it, revelling in the new sensations of pain and pleasure.

Christine and I worked fast. We kicked off our shoes and pulled off our socks. Then tied Dr Herges' wrists and ankles to the bedposts with the long white socks. He was securely trussed up before he even knew what had happened, still wallowing in the beating he'd taken, rubbing his pulped bum against the bed.

I reached down and pulled his gown up to his chest, revealing his cock. It was stretched out long and hard on his flat, hairy belly. The man's glassy eyes came back into focus, as Christine and I stared down at his hard-on, grinning. He looked from me to Christine, at the ties binding his arms. He rattled the bed with his arms and legs, fear flashing in his brown eyes for the first time we'd ever seen.

'What – what are you girls up to?' he said, lifting his head, leaving his mortarboard behind on the pillow.

'Oh, just about anything, Dr Herges,' I teased, taking his erection in hand and giving it a quick stroke.

He groaned, his compact body jumping. I handed his pulsing cock over to Christine, and she tugged on it, her red nails biting into the smooth shaft. Then she dropped it, and slapped it.

The swollen appendage flipped towards me, sprung back again. I smacked it flat on Dr Herges' stomach. He bucked. I backhanded his cock, my own glossy red fingernails scraping over his skin. Christine smacked it back again, and we batted the man's hard-on back and forth, the thing lengthening, thickening, becoming even more rigid.

Dr Herges rolled his head from side to side on the pillow, enjoying each and every blow, his shaft reddening, streaks flashing around his groin where our nails scratched him.

Then we two school-uniformed girls climbed onto the headmaster's bed in our bare feet. I sat on his stomach, Christine on his thighs, facing one another, Dr Herges' twitching cock between us. He struggled only half-heartedly, Christine and I riding his heaving stomach and trembling legs, our bare bottoms burning into his heated skin.

We scooched closer together on the tied-up man, closer to his straining prick. Our skirts hiked up even higher and we scissored our legs together like we had so many times in our dorm room, and then in our cheap apartment downtown. Only this time, there was a tall cock between us, our moist, furry pussies pressing into its beating shaft on either side.

We moved our hips, undulating our pelvises, rubbing together against that erection.

'Fuck, yes!' Dr Herges shouted, thrusting upwards, uttering the first swear words we'd ever heard from the distinguished academic.

I clutched his hairy chest and clawed at his rigid, pink nipples from behind, staring at Christine, pushing my pussy against his cock and her cunt. She gripped Dr Herges' knees and glared at me, rubbing back, breasts jumping underneath her open blouse.

We're just light little things, but the bed groaned with the combined weights of our shifting bodies, and the groaning Dr Herges. We moved faster, muscles in our legs rippling, stomachs tightened, slickened pussies rubbing vigorously against that fur-sandwiched cock.

'Fuck, girls!' Dr Herges cried, bucking beneath us. Sperm leapt out of his pussy-buffed cock in great geysering ropes, over and over. He streaked our stomachs and our fur with his ecstasy, shooting off a gallon.

Christine shrieked and shuddered, coming herself, her pussy jumping against Dr Herges' spouting cock. The girl was jolted by multiple orgasms, squirting her joy, pretty face contorted with lust.

I bit my lip and tried to hold off, and couldn't. Wet, wild orgasm went off in my rubbing muff and rolled through my quivering body. I gushed all over Dr Herges' cock, buffeted by wave after wave of utter bliss, carrying me away.

It took only a few minutes for the great scholar to figure out what was going on. 'You're robbing me,' he stated correctly.

Christine had pulled a leather suitcase out of his closet, and we were busy packing it with any items of value we could find in his bedroom. Before we hit his study, where we'd heard there were a number of valuable books and objects of art, not to mention a strongbox full of gold coins.

I glanced down at the man on the bed. He looked a sorry sight tied up like that, stripped of most of his academic attire and all of his authority, flaccid cock curled up in its nest of black pubes.

'That's right, Dr Herges,' I replied. 'We put on our old school uniforms just for the occasion – to fit in on campus again. We were actually expecting you to be at the graduation ceremony; I just rang the doorbell as a precaution.' I shrugged. 'But since you were home, we had to improvise. And now, after all that's happened, I doubt if you're even going to report this robbery.'

I grinned at the man. 'Pretty smart on our feet, aren't we, Dr Herges?'

'And off,' Christine added, smiling, as well.

Rough Justice
by Beverly Langland

POLICEWOMAN 5727 STEPPED INTO the dark side of the alley and lit a cigarette, leaving me trembling and feeling more exposed than I had ever felt. Incredibly, I still held my skirt high, revealing my lace panties for her inspection. They felt so delicate now, offering me little protection against the depredation of her eyes. I could feel the chill of the cool night air gently teasing my sex, could feel the telltale wet patch the policewoman's actions had made me produce. I stood exactly as she had left me, feeling light-headed and confused. I pushed back against the wall to steady my trembling thighs, drawing in great breaths of air until my giddiness faded – although the confusion remained. I didn't know what I should do next. Policewoman 5727 leaned against the opposite wall, smoking casually, considering the spectacle of me dressed in a parody of a policewoman's attire, taking in the pathetic image I presented. She didn't seem amused with my choice of uniform.

I believe I showed considerable control under the circumstances. Truth was I wanted to cry but felt that would only make me appear more girlish than I already felt. Leaving me exposed in this way had left a strange taste in my mouth. It took some time before recognition dawned. With horror I realised the taste in my mouth was the tang of disappointment.

I didn't know what I had done wrong. One minute I danced with the other girls, the next a burly bouncer with a suspect moustache plucked me bodily from the dance floor. He carried me kicking and screaming towards the main foyer next to the nightclub's exit. My mind was all a jumble. One minute I yelled, protesting my innocence, the next a bout of the giggles laid me speechless. I admit that since I was on my hen weekend I didn't take my "capture" too seriously. I felt certain that Carol or one of the other girls had set me up. However, once we reached the foyer I wasn't so certain. The bouncer dutifully handed me over to the awaiting police officers. Two of them stood like stone statues, their faces expressionless. A hunk of a man, muscles abound, who barely fit his crisp uniform and a brutish-looking woman, also Amazonian in proportion. The man who I had mistakenly assumed would turn out to be a stripper clearly didn't speak much English. He left the talking to the woman. She wore a stern face and spoke to me in short, guttural sentences. Her face so stern I couldn't look into her eyes or stop laughing. For some reason, the fact that I was also dressed as a raunchy "copper" had me in stitches. Instead, I stared at her epaulette, which announced her to be policewoman 5727. It didn't help that she spoke at me not to me. The only words I understood clearly were my own name, which the policewoman repeated. 'Samantha Brooks?' she asked again, not quite getting the pronunciation correct. Not knowing what they expected of me, I nodded.

Nodding turned out to be a big mistake. The next thing I knew, the two giants had grabbed me under my arms and all but frogmarched me across the cobbled square outside the nightclub. I felt bewildered. My arrest no longer felt like a silly prank at all. I continued to protest the best I could, but neither of my captors took notice. I tried to explain in Pidgin English, but they wouldn't even let me go back for my handbag in which I rather stupidly had left my passport. I knew I *should* have kept it secure in the hotel. In desperation, I tried looking for help from my friends, but I couldn't see them anywhere. Surely one of them had seen the bouncer pick me up? Why hadn't they followed? The square was still busy, even in the early hours and soon the three of us were lost in the throng of people. No one seemed concerned about my abduction. They assumed as I had that I had done something wrong. But what? We went marching onwards, past what looked to me like the local police station, until the crowds had thinned. I'm not a violent person, but I could feel my anger rising. To suffer the ignominy of arrest. I paled when I realised what that would mean. I would be up in front of a magistrate. That would put an end to any prospect I aspired to of a career in law. Besides, what would my fiancé Gareth think?

Like me, you may have seen images on reality television shows of brazen young women, drunk, fighting in the street after a night on the town. Their disgraceful behaviour had always appalled me. Now, incredibly, I had become one of them. I suppose I *was* a trifle drunk. More because I rarely drank rather than by consuming an excess. OK, I *had* been in a fight. Well, more an altercation with my chief bridesmaid who had promised faithfully to look after me, who promised there would be no "dodgy" encounters with strange men. I lost my temper when I realised the truth. For a moment only. Surely, that couldn't be the only reason for my arrest. Besides, Carol would never have reported me, if only for the fact that she wouldn't like losing face. She's a much bigger girl than I am. I actually bounced off when I flung myself at her in my rage. The sight of me falling arse over tit made everyone laugh, including Carol and me. We soon forgot our spat, or so I had thought.

The police officers led me away from the crowds, along what suspiciously appeared to be a shady back alley. So it turned out to be. For the first time I grew concerned. Too late. As soon as I realised the alley was indeed a dead-end, the policewoman tightened her grip and pushed me roughly against the brick wall, squashing me flat. She searched me, or at least made a futile attempt. The search seemed pointless since I only wore a few scraps of clothing. Police officer 5727 searched me all the same, adding to my growing suspicion that they weren't genuine police officers. The big woman wasn't gentle. Deliberately so, I thought. I started to protest and found my face cruelly pushed against the rough brickwork for my effort. 'Now look here!' I tried to protest again, but the policewoman would hear nothing of it. 'Quiet!' she barked, with such ferocity that for the first time my apprehension verged on fear. They had me down an unknown alley in a strange city. I was alone and at the mercy of two burly strangers. *Alone!* I couldn't understand why the other girls had abandoned me. OK, my abductors were purportedly police officers but they were behaving in a profoundly un-police-like manner. Besides the gleaming numbers on their epaulettes, they had shown me no official identification. Only their edge of authority kept me from running.

I managed to quell my shaking as the policewoman spread my legs lewdly, then continued the search. I had never been manhandled in this way, had never been so ignominiously treated. Certainly not by a woman. It had been a day of fun and frolic. Although not drunk, I had had a tad more than usual and I still wore a flush of excitement from all the dancing. My arrest made for a sad ending to a wonderful day. To cap it all I could hardly believe the policewoman's rough handling had me aroused. Damn my imagination! I occasionally felt benign lesbian urges, but instead of soft warmth and gentle lips, I had this bully. I knew the alcohol had caused the fuzziness in my head. I should never have mixed my drinks. Normally a careful and responsible drinker, it seemed unfair now that the first time I had drunk in excess, the police had arrested me. Moreover, for what? I still didn't know specifically what I had done wrong.

The hulk of the policeman stood to one side making no

pretence of turning away or averting his eyes as the policewoman searched me. I didn't think I could be more humiliated. Policewoman 5727, obviously enjoyed her work. Her hands were everywhere, feeling my breasts, reaching under my short pleated skirt. I felt certain my treatment and the search in particular wasn't standard procedure. I wondered again if the other girls had set me up. On the other hand, were these two taking advantage of a foreign girl on an otherwise quiet night? I bit my lip as cold hands reached my bottom, uncertain what I should do. I was in enough trouble and I felt my safety depended on how I responded. If I complained, it could make matters worse. Worse? What was I thinking? What could be worse than being touched up by a butch policewoman down some dark alley?

I soon found out. The policewoman spun me around by my shoulders, almost making me fall off of my high-heels. Only now, tinged with anger and a sense of injustice did I keep my chin raised, staring directly into the woman's dark menacing eyes. She wore an infuriating smirk. Oh, how I would have liked to smack that face! 'Lift skirt,' she said, reinforcing her request with the gesture of laying her palms flat and curling her fingers. My mouth dropped, uncertain I had heard the woman correctly. It seemed incredulous that she would say such a thing. 'Whatever for?' I asked.

Then again, I wasn't in England I reminded myself. The policewoman stared at me intently. I could see that she wasn't in any mood to justify her actions. 'Because I say,' her only concession.

I shook my head. No way would I do such a thing. Not there. Not in the alley with the blond hulk driving me crazy as he watched with that stupid inane grin. 'No!'

Policewoman 5727 took a deep breath drawing up to her full height. It was only then that I realised just how big the woman was. She leaned closer, and wriggled her fingers in front of my face. 'You prefer hands, yes?'

No I didn't. I shook my head again, but she made it blatantly clear that what I wanted didn't count for much. 'Yes, you like,' the policewoman continued. 'I hear you moan when I touch. You enjoy too much, so now, no hands.' She turned to the waiting policeman and said something in Russian or whatever language the two spoke. I was never good at geography or languages. They both turned my way and laughed, which only made me angrier. I wasn't moaning when she touched me, was I? *Not in that way, surely.* 'If you think I enjoy being manhandled like a piece of meat–'

The policewoman's glare stopped me short. I could tell by the look on her face that she had lost patience. 'Hurry. We not got all night,' she snapped.

I tried one last plea. 'You can't seriously expect me to lift my skirt?'

'Do I look like joking? Up, up! Unless tart have something to hide?'

'I'm not a tart,' I protested, but I did have something to hide. The policewoman's air of dominance and my sense of helplessness had me aroused. It shouldn't be so, I know, but the truth of the matter was that her rough handling had. I was terrified my arousal would be visible, but even more worried what would happen if I refused to lift my skirt. Therefore, I tentatively reached for the hem of my loose pleated skirt and slowly – reluctantly – pulled upwards. I noticed the policeman smile as I revealed my lace panties. God only knows why I chose to wear them. They were fit for the bedroom only. In my submission, I tried to avoid the policewoman's eyes, but her hand was on my face, her strong fingers squeezing my cheeks and lifting my chin. Then, with her eyes firmly fixed on mine, she drew her nightstick from her belt, and held the black baton high, making certain I saw what she held. My first thought, inappropriate considering the circumstances, was that it was like a huge black penis. The police couldn't have chosen a more phallic weapon if they'd tried.

Then the nightstick disappeared out of sight and I felt the cold plastic brush against my leg. Slowly the policewoman moved the baton higher, past my knee, grazing the inside of my thighs until the coldness of the plastic nestled firmly against my sex. I gasped in surprise. The baton felt cold and hard. So very hard. Policewoman 5727 smiled at my unspoken protest then pulled the baton higher, almost lifting me onto my toes. I panicked. Surely, she didn't mean to ...

Yet, she did! The policewoman started sawing the baton back and forth, keeping the hard plastic tight against the crevice of my sex. My labia peeled under the pressure. Despite my trepidation, I felt my arousal growing. 5727 made it difficult for me not to become aroused. I hated the idea of enjoying what this woman did to me, but the evidence in the gusset of my panties refuted any claim I made to the contrary. I was wet. No, I was soaking. I blushed with the realisation, my cheeks flaming red as I imperceptibly pushed against the hardness between my legs, hoping that the policewoman wouldn't notice. What was I doing? Suddenly the baton and the wonderful pressure disappeared, and that's how she left me. In a state of arousal.

Eventually she ended my torment. Policewoman 5727 pointed to the left, back towards the cobbled square. 'This way police station,' she said, and then she pointed to the right, further into the alleyway. 'This way freedom. You choose!'

By freedom, I knew policewoman 5727 meant something different altogether. I wasn't drunk enough not to understand what was going on here. I weighed up my options. I couldn't risk ending up with a criminal record and forever lose the opportunity of practising law. I remained undecided. As if sensing my nervousness, 5727 sent the burly policeman away. He walked out of the alleyway without protest. I felt relieved to see him go. At least now, I could rule him out of the equation. Take the policewoman's alternative punishment, whatever that may be, or ... I couldn't even contemplate the alternative. 'I'll come with you,' I said. 5727 smiled. She showed a magnificent set of pearly-white teeth. 'Good!' She took my arm and marched me deeper into the alleyway. I didn't protest until she unhooked the handcuffs from her belt and I realised what sort of punishment she intended.

'Now wait a minute!' I protested.

'Changed mind?' she said coolly.

I shook my head, not believing how events had unfolded. I had to let this brute of a lesbian punish me in some dark alley while my so-called friends danced and enjoyed themselves just the other side of the square. 'No.' I hadn't.

'Open top,' she said pointing at my blouse.

Whereas lifting my skirt had been embarrassing, I was now entering a completely new class of humiliation. My ritual undressing was plainly sexual. There was no doubt in my mind now. I was willingly selling my body in return for 5727's clemency. I was selling my body to a stranger. I no longer felt the same apprehension I'd felt earlier. Something stronger had usurped it. Excitement. I liked the notion of selling myself cheap this way. There was something base about the idea. Yet, I told myself I didn't have a choice. Policewoman 5727 had forced me into this humiliating situation, and I liked her air of dominance. I undid the buttons one by one, taking my time. I could see the lust in 5727's eyes as she followed the progress of my fingers. I realised that in some small way I held a spell over her, just as she had over me. I pulled the folds apart, revealing my lace bra. Endowed I'm not, but my breasts are firm and my nipples are long and responsive. I could feel them stiffen even before they came into view.

I didn't wait for 5727 to tell me to open my bra. I unhooked the front catch and pulled the cups aside. My nipples grew taut in the chill evening air, much to the delight of my captor. She stubbed her cigarette on the side of her boot, threw the fag end into the bin, and then stepped forward. I had to fight the urge to flee even at this late stage. Was it too late to back out? She took my breasts in her large hands, feeling their weight, and then ran the ends of her thumbs across the tips of my nipples. A shock of electricity shot through my body. It was just a simple touch, but it felt like much more, as if I had crossed a forbidden line. It wasn't the first time a girl had touched my breasts, but I had never felt anything like this. Why should that be? I didn't have much time to ponder as 5727 crushed my nipples between finger and thumb. Pain shot through me where moments before there had been pleasure. Despite the pain, I groaned and the tingling sensation inside my panties grew.

Then without warning, 5727 spun me around again and pushed me against the rough brick wall. She spread and lifted my arms above my head, making sure she flattened my breasts against the wall. She pressed the flat of her palm into my back making certain I could feel the rough brickwork on my exposed flesh. Then she lifted my skirt and tucked the hem into the waistband. I grew nervous as I waited for the big woman to pull down my knickers as I felt certain she would. However, she made me wait. I'm not quite sure how long exactly, but despite the trepidation growing within me I wanted to get on with it. I shook my head, not believing I thought 'on with it' and not 'get it over with'. Soon afterwards, I felt her large hands on my bottom, feeling, stroking with pleasure. I felt fingertips in the waistband and then in one fell swoop my panties lay about my ankles.

Policewoman 5727 tapped her foot at the side of my shoes, urging me to spread my legs. She kept tapping until I could feel the lace material of my panties strain against my ankles. I heard 5727 slowly pull the leather belt out of the loops of her trousers. I tried to see what she intended to do with it. I couldn't see, but I didn't need to, as my imagination worked overtime. A terrifying crack rent the air. No pain accompanied the noise so I guessed she had folded the belt in half and smacked the palm of her hand to make certain I knew what would follow next. I trembled while I waited for the worst, anticipation pumping adrenaline through my body. 'You bad girl,' 5727 said in her broken English. 'Now you have spanking.'

Without further ado, she brought the belt down hard. The crack of it hitting my exposed bottom seemed as loud as a gunshot in the confined space, the sharp sound reverberating between the alley walls. Shocked by how much the first strike hurt, I squealed on impact. Paying no heed, 5727 brought the belt down again, this time on the other cheek, this time a little harder. Having warmed both cheeks, she then began to spank me repeatedly. I squealed with each blow, certain my cries could be heard at least as far as the square. Surely, someone would come to investigate. Nobody did. I didn't know at the time that the blond hulk had stationed himself at the entrance to the alleyway as a deterrent. After the initial pounding of my bottom, 5727 stood back to examine her handiwork. Tears streamed down my face. She took hold of my chin and turned my face slightly, perhaps making certain I shed real tears. They certainly were. The flesh of my bottom was on fire!

Perhaps 5727 took pity on me then, for she didn't resume my punishment. I don't know if she originally intended to, but I was grateful she didn't. I didn't realise just how grateful until I felt her large hands press against my blazing bottom. She curled one finger into the crease of my buttocks, trawling the wetness of my soaking pussy backwards. A soft groan escaped my lips. I had no idea why, but I wanted the bitch to touch me, right where the heat was most intense. At my centre, deep inside my cunt. It wasn't simply that I felt horny. It *had* to be her. It had to be this particular butch female who had just given me the hiding of my life. Don't ask me to explain. I can't. Logic had nothing to do with it. Nor fear, because I felt strangely comfortable in her hands, letting her fondle me as she pleased. Just as I grew accustomed to the fondling, she changed focus and slipped a finger into my anus. God, it felt so big inside me. For a moment at least, I forgot about the heat in my bottom.

I felt 5727 change position. For one insane moment, I thought she was preparing to fuck me with her gruesome-looking nightstick. I had visions of her cruelly impaling me. My heart raced, making my pussy flood in anticipation. Or fear. A little of both perhaps. The wanton in me wanted her to use the beast; the sane part of me urged caution. In the end, it wasn't the nightstick I felt but her tongue. She spread my buttocks and started probing, licking across my anus as if it were the most natural of things. At first, I was shocked, and then I quickly grew to like the sensation. She tugged on my bottom cheeks, searching now for my pussy. Groans emanated from between my legs as she strived towards her target. I could sense how excited she was and her excitement drove my own arousal.

I backed away from the wall so I could bend. As I bent forward, 5727 followed me with her tongue, delving deeper as I made myself more available. My fingernails raked against the rough brickwork of the wall as I tried to hold on to reality. The thrashing of 5727's tongue grew more frantic the more I moaned. We drove each other on without uttering a word. There was only one destination and we were heading straight for it. 5727 continued to fuck me quickly, her tongue driving deep as she slowly worked her way forward. I let go of the wall and slid one hand behind her head forcing her deeper. I no longer knew who was in control. It didn't matter. We were no longer fighting each other.

A squeal of pleasure escaped my mouth as 5727 finally reached my clitoris. She flicked the throbbing nubbin as viciously as she had attacked my bottom with the belt. It seemed 5727 didn't take prisoners. Once she had me wriggling on the end of her tongue, stopping wasn't an option. I moaned breathily, grinding my sex against her, smothering her face with my juices, pushing so hard the ridge of her nose entered my sex. I grabbed a handful of her hair and pulled, the pleasure rising steadily inside me. 5727's tongue darted all over me, teasing my clit, occasionally sliding back over my anus, then pushing forward again, keeping me guessing, letting me know that she remained in control after all. I couldn't think of anything except the feel of 5727's amazing mouth on me. I cried out, my legs beginning to falter as I started to come. My breath turned ragged as the unmistakeable surge of orgasm swept over me. 5727 kept lapping, emptying me until I could barely stand I felt so drained. I tried to move away from her savage tongue, but she held me tight, continuing to lash at my clit until the inflamed flesh hurt so much I came a second time.

Afterwards, policewoman 5727 stood gathering herself. I fell back against her, exhausted. She kissed my neck softly. Her first real sign of intimacy.

The girls were waiting for me at the entrance of the alley. Some of them were chatting to the hulk in the policeman's uniform. He answered them in perfect accented English. My initial confusion lifted as realisation dawned. One of the bitches *had* set me up! Carol probably. As my chief bridesmaid, I had pleaded with her not to let me fall into a cheap one-night stand. I suppose she had kept her word. A big girl, Carol had been my "protector" during most of my teenage years. We were so close I was the first person she admitted being a lesbian to. Of course, I knew she had designs on my body and, once or twice, I had given in to her persistence. Nevertheless, I wasn't like her. I loved Gareth. He was a wonderful lover and I looked forward to becoming his wife.

Carol had an absurd grin on her face, so I knew that she knew exactly what had happened down that dark alley. I blushed crimson as it belatedly dawned on me that all of the girls must also know. At least the gist if not the details. Carol came to me, placing her arm around my waist. 'Come on, the night is still young,' she said. The other girls screamed with delight and we all headed back towards the nightclub. Out of sight of everyone else, Carol's hand lazily dropped to my bottom and she gave my sore cheeks a gentle squeeze. I knew then that despite my continued reluctance, she would make me hers eventually. My mind raced ahead to events that seemed beyond my control. Gareth or Carol? Neither would give me up without a fight. I didn't know what would happen once we returned to England. Interesting times lay ahead. Despite the turmoil raging in my head, I was looking forward to the battle.

An Itch to Scratch
by Tara S Nichols

I'VE NEVER HAD A *thing* before – you know, sexually. Some people – they like firemen, others – they like feet, but me, I'm pretty casual. That is until that smoking hot nurse in the overly starched white uniform walked into the clinic waiting room. It was late on Halloween, and I sat on my vinyl chair, sandwiched between a Wookie and a Stormtrooper. The mood in the lobby was rather dull, with the exception of a green-faced witch who winked at me from across the room. I couldn't tell if she was giving me the evil eye or trying to be seductive, and I couldn't decide if the oozing wounds on the Frankenbride to my left were real or if she was an expert with make-up.

I wore what I always wore; jeans: a T-shirt and sneakers. I hated Halloween; an excuse of a holiday for sappy losers to pretend they were six again.

I could have happily maintained that level of scorn, too, if it hadn't been for that nurse. My firm belief in Halloween had been blown to smithereens.

With lips pursed and painted fire-engine red, she was a curvaceous stereotype of everything nurse-fantasy. A bold red cross drew the eye to her left breast, then down into her gaping neckline to her swollen cleavage. Carrying a clipboard in her hand, she strode up to the front counter and leaned across the high platform. As she raised herself up on tippytoes, the short skirt of her uniform came just below the luscious curve of her bottom. Either she was blissfully unaware of her near exposure, or she didn't care that the entire waiting room now knew the colour of her underwear.

Another nurse on the receptionist side pushed a form in front of the short-skirted nurse. The other woman made a few marks on the sheet with a pen and the two of them conferred for a while, about what, I don't know. I was too busy sizing up her long, slender, white stocking-clad legs.

Then the receptionist called a name and the vampire to my right stood up and followed the receptionist down the back hall. The hot nurse reached for another file and in doing so her skirt rose another inch. I swear an audible inhalation of breath in perfect sync could be heard throughout the room. After reading a few names the hot nurse turned around and pointed to me.

'Jess Ingman?' she asked. I shook my head, feeling disappointed. Frankenbride stood hopefully.

She frowned and read the list again.

'Alex Fields, then?'

I nodded.

'Come with me,' she said firmly, and the Frankenbride sat back down.

The Wookie gave me what I assumed was a congratulatory pat on the shoulder and I tried to hide my smile as I followed after the hot nurse.

'The hospital is a little crowded because of the holiday.' She spoke over her shoulder as we walked. 'Seeing as you are one of the only ones not bleeding, do you mind a rather unorthodox office in which to conduct your exam?'

'No. No, I don't mind at all,' I stammered, pulling my mind off of her pert little ass long enough to answer. 'But I'm just here for a prescription refill.'

She stopped walking and checked her charts. 'Hmm, so you are, but it also says here to do the standard physical exam, just to be sure you're not just ...' Her words dropped away and a slight blush coloured her cheeks.

'I'm not what?'

'Some people *like* taking pills, Mr Fields.' Her eyebrows arched expectantly.

I suddenly got her drift. They wanted to make sure I wasn't a user. 'Oh, I assure you that's not the case.' I gave her one of my best winning smiles.

'Glad to hear it.' Her lips stretched into a tight line as she opened the door to the supply room. I looked beyond her outstretched arm, a grand gesture where one might have thought she was ushering me into a palace, not a small dull grey room that hosted a sink, shelves loaded with supplies, and had a pungent smell of Band-Aids mingled with disinfectants. Even though she'd warned me, I still felt shocked.

'Wow, you weren't kidding,' I said turning around just in time to see her shut the door. It closed with an ominous click.

'Now, if you'll take your shirt and pants off,' she said walking past me with her eyes on the clipboard. 'Then you can hop up onto that gurney.' She pointed to the bed on wheels that had been tucked in behind the door.

'For real?' I scoffed, still unable to comprehend the necessity of such an exam.

She lowered the clipboard and speared me with a level look. 'Would you rather take this up with one of the doctors then?' I could see I'd pushed a button. This was a sore spot and her anger simmered close to the surface. She seemed perturbed by my insolence, as though I were only the one hundredth patient to underestimate her that day.

I glanced at her golden cleavage and decided it could be worse. I could be trapped in a storage room with some ugly old geezer. At least I'd be undressing in front of a babe.

'Have it your way.' I grinned and tried to make light of my blunder, but she wasn't having any of it. She also didn't look the other way while I undressed. My fingers found the hem of my shirt and I swallowed hard, knowing her eyes were on me. I'd undressed in front of plenty of women before, yet this one seemed different, almost judgemental.

It was then that I noticed the white gauze bandage on her wrist. A little pink tinge told me her wound was recent and it had started to seep.

'You might want to see a doctor yourself.'

She rolled her eyes, impatient with me again. 'I'm a nurse. This is nothing I can't take care of.'

'I'll bet you can take care of quite a bit,' I said with a chuckle as my pants fell to my ankles, and then I cringed, thinking I sounded corny enough to deserve a smack. To my surprise a slight smile flicked at the corner of her mouth.

I swung my legs up onto the gurney and lay down on my back. Her clipboard bumped the metal tray beside me as she closed the distance and a warm breeze filled with her spicy perfume wafted past my nose. I closed my eyes for a moment, breathing in the intoxicating scent.

I opened them a second later when I felt her warm hands on my inner thigh, right at the bottom of my boxers. My cock twitched in response and I held my breath, willing it to stay down.

'What is this light red patch?' She scrunched up her nose as she prodded my skin. Even though I thought her squeamishness made her look cuter than all hell, I wondered at her tolerance. Shouldn't a nurse have a better poker face, or in the very least, recognise the symptoms of a Poison Ivy reaction?

Every time she poked me, it itched. 'Yeah. That would be the rash I came in about. It's almost cleared up,' I said though gritted teeth.

Her eyes went wide. She pulled back quickly and reached for a box of gloves. 'Is it contagious?'

'It's Poison Ivy. Shouldn't you know?'

Obvious relief washed over her pretty features and I saw the stern mask slip back on. 'Of course I know. I hadn't read the whole chart, that's all.'

Her fingertips returned to my warm thigh and cringed as

the cool latex grazed my skin. The thin cloth of my boxers lifted, creating a breeze and I raised my head off the pillow in surprise.

'What are you doing?'

'These will have to come off. I need to have a closer look.'

'Why?'

'You wouldn't want it to spread, would you?'

Spread? My anxiety spiked another notch higher. I'd already endured two weeks with the itchy blisters down the entire length of my legs, and believe me, the thought that it might spread just two inches higher to my sac was enough to keep me up at night. 'Do you think it could do that?'

She tsk-tsked and flashed me a sugary smile. 'There's only one way to be certain, honey.'

I could recognise when I was being placated, but under the circumstances, I figured I owed her the benefit of the doubt. Before I could debate it any farther, her fingers slipped beneath the waistband of my shorts and with a mighty jerk, she tugged them down. My face burned with embarrassment as her gaze fell upon my now rock hard cock.

A sly smile crept over her face.

'Well now that just won't do.' She clicked her tongue against her teeth again and my discomfort deepened.

'How can I be expected to see anything with you looking like this?' She turned and focused her attention on a shelf behind her.

'Like what? What's wrong?' I asked not bothering to hide the panic in my voice.

When she turned around again she held a small shaver and a bottle of hand soap. 'It's nothing to worry about. Just a quick touch up.'

'You're going to shave me?' I blathered.

'Most certainly.' I heard the water running and the sound of a cup being filled. She returned to me, razor held out ready. 'It will be over before you know it. Just don't move.'

I held as still as I could but when her palm wrapped around the end of my cock I jumped. She gripped me tighter and I felt the warm soapy lather spread across my sac. It was rather pleasant until I realised she'd brought the razor down on my skin as well. I held my breath until she'd rendered me hairless.

'There,' she said sounding satisfied. She set the razor down but didn't let go of my cock. It pulsed like a heartbeat and raised itself up in a mutinous attempt to get closer to her. To make matters worse she brought her face down for a closer inspection of the area. I could feel her hot breath against my naked sac, and when I raised my head to look, I had a perfect view down her blouse. Her breasts hung full, yet low, and I had no doubt she wasn't wearing a bra. They swung heavily with each minor move and I imagined how good it would feel to suck on each nipple. My cock twitched under her hand and her eyebrows arched in surprise.

She frowned and straightened, her gaze fixated on my cock the whole time. Then, with a curious tilt to her head, she slid her palm up and down my shaft.

'Does it hurt when I do this?'

I was struck by her official tone.

'No.' I barely managed to answer. 'Not at all.'

She shifted her hand to a new position but continued to manhandle my cock.

'How about now?'

'No, that's still very nice.'

She paused. 'Not to alarm you, but I'm worried. It has turned a deep purple, you see, and I'd like to make sure it's not sensitive.'

'Oh, it's sensitive,' I said with a chuckle. First, she revealed a startling ignorance in regards to Poison Ivy, and now she seemed unbelievably innocent about a man's physical response to heavy petting.

She tapped one fingernail on her front teeth, and pondered my erection. 'I'll have to do further tests.'

Before I could inquire about what kind of tests she intended to do, she brought her brightly painted lips to the head of my cock. My eyes went wide.

'I'm going to check how it does under pressure.'

I threw my head back against the pillow as the heat of her mouth surrounded my cock. Her lips formed a tight seal around my rigid flesh and her tongue moved across the shaft, wetting it before she sucked it all the way in, right to the back of her throat. My fingers gripped the edge of the bed and I groaned like a man having an amputation without an anaesthetic. She began to bob up and down the entire length, drawing blood away from all my other extremities. My gums began to tingle as it rushed along my shaft to the tip of my prick.

I stole a glance to see her hard at work, her face distorted and stretched at an oddly beautiful angle, the brilliant trail of red lipstick that had transferred onto my skin like a bright red gash out of some B-grade horror movie, and the dishevelled state her crisp uniform had become, and I nearly ruptured like Old Faithful.

I was certain she intended to work me over good, until she abruptly left off my cock and came to stand by my shoulder. Dragging the back of her hand across her lipstick-smeared mouth, she wiped away what was left of her make-up, then reached into her hip pocket, pulled out a shiny metal container, and applied a fresh coat.

'Your pressure is good.' She popped the cap back on the lipstick, and addressed me as though nothing out of the ordinary just happened. 'Stamina too. But I'd like to do one more test just to be sure.'

I nodded in agreement, feeling too blissed-out, too shocked, to do much of anything else. Only when I heard the sharp tearing of paper did I think to question what the next test might be.

A moment later she returned to the juncture of my legs. Craning my neck, I watched as she ran the pad of her thumb over the little hole in the end of my cock, smearing the drop of liquid that had appeared there into my skin, and then rolled a condom down the length of my shaft.

'What could this possibly have to do with a prescription for steroids?' I dared to ask.

She just smiled and raised the bottom of her skirt to the middle of her waist, revealing crisp white lacy panties and equally white garters. I watched in amazement as she peeled the rest of the uniform off and stared at her in stunned silence upon sight of her glorious naked breasts. Her nipples hardened into tight pink spikes before my eyes. I moved to go to her but she pressed me back down onto the bed with a hand in the middle of my chest.

'Not so fast.' Her eyes burned with desire. 'I'm not done with you yet.'

'Thank heavens,' I said with a laugh and let my head flop back down onto the bed.

She climbed up onto the gurney and swung a leg over top of me. I placed my hands on her tits and began to massage them gently, pleased to see she didn't resist. They were firm, full, tanned, and all natural, and she moaned as I squeezed them. My mouth watered and I longed to suck them, but I soon learned she had other plans. Reaching between us, she guided the head of my cock up and through what I had thought was the crotch of her panties. I realised, after I'd breached all possible barriers, that she wore crotchless panties. I watched with awe and admiration as she began to rock her hips, catching a glimpse of her pink cleft beneath the lacy white fabric from time to time.

She ground down onto me as though she couldn't get enough, throwing her head back, and obviously enjoying the feeling of me inside her. I knew full well she was getting more than enough the way my head drove into her cervix, yet she bore down with everything she had. Her breasts bounced and swung as we pounded her end. The gurney groaned with her ambitious movements until I feared someone might come to investigate from all the noise we were making.

I reached for her, bringing her breasts to my mouth, sucking one nipple, then both at once, until she moaned with pleasure. I swirled my tongue across each tight bud and felt my cock fatten again. She groaned her appreciation loudly, bucking her hips down onto me, slamming each thrust home, and I realised she'd reached her peak. Raising my hips, I matched her thrusts with wild abandon, drawing out her orgasm with my own carnal need. I swear I tested that rubber's elasticity when I came, even uttering a guttural growl.

I lay on the gurney, my mind far away, my nose full of sex and the weight of a gorgeous, half naked woman sprawled out on top of me. I was only vaguely aware when she began to move, to get dressed, and clean up the mess we'd made around us. When she stood by my side once again I forced my eyelids to stay open, to see the white starched uniform, another new coat of red paint on her sensuous mouth, and a notepad and pen in her hand.

'What's that?' I asked, seeing her writing something out.

'Your prescription,' she said with a sweet smile.

'My perscrip–' I cut off.

'You passed all the tests – with flying colours, I must add. You can get dressed now and see yourself out.' She pressed the note into my flaccid hand and picked up her clipboard.

She'd opened the door and was already down the hall before I thought to go after her. Dressing quickly I barrelled down the hall and burst into the waiting room but there was no sign of her.

'Bloody hell,' I cursed, feeling shocked and dismayed.

A receptionist from behind the counter looked up. 'Sir?

May I help you?'

'Did you see a nurse come through here recently?'

The receptionist gave me a look. 'Yeah, lots of them.'

'This one was different. She had a big red cross over her left breast, bright red lipstick and pumps.'

'We don't have a nurse that goes by that description.' She frowned. 'What is your name? Maybe that will tell me something.'

'Alex Fields.' I offered absentmindedly.

The receptionist looked up sharp. 'Mr Fields? Bloody hell! We've been calling your name for the last 20 minutes.' She pursed her lips and plunked a vial full of pills up on the counter. 'Honestly, I had you pegged for the most impatient patient in the world when I saw that you had already gone.' She laughed now and shook her head. 'The doctor filled your prescription within minutes of your arrival.'

I looked at the vial.

'Then who was–' I looked at the note in my hand. Opening it up I read the phone number my pretty little nurse had inscribed.

'Come to think of it ...' the receptionist rapped her pen against the side of her head, deep in thought. 'There was a patient in here going by the description.'

I looked to the receptionist, then to the vial. With a hasty apology I snatched up my medicine and raced out the doors. If I was lucky I might be able to catch my nurse waiting for the elevator. If I did, I might even be able to convince her I was a doctor and she was in dire need of a check-up.

The Deal
by Sadie Wolf

I'D WANTED TO LEAVE him for a while but his fingers were in so many pies and my fingers were interlaced with his. Life with him had seemed so glamorous at first; everyone in the city knew him and being involved in stuff that was against the law was exciting. I embraced my new life and did a pretty thorough job of burning my old one. I lost touch with friends and the road back to respectability began to seem further and further away.

But three years in, the shine began to tarnish. A little voice started up in my head; I don't know if it was some in-built self preservation instinct or the voice of my mother but something was telling me I was worth more than the life I was living.

At the same time, it had slowly begun to dawn on me that I didn't find him as attractive as I used to. Maybe it was the way he was never wholly sober and his breath always smelled of alcohol and roll-ups. Maybe it was the way he had recently developed a paunch and a double chin just as I was beginning to discover the hitherto unknown joys of exercise. But whatever it was, the shine was fading. I began to dream of being rescued.

I hadn't thought as far as actually *leaving* him – our lives were so entwined that I was unable to imagine actually embarking on a life without him, let alone actually initiating the messy, difficult, painful break-up process. But I began to hope that something, or someone, would come along and save me.

Rescue did come but it wasn't in the shape I had imagined and I did not escape messiness, difficulty or pain. In fact, what I went through was way more difficult and painful than if I had just had the guts to tell him it was over and walk away. And messy. What I went through in order to earn my freedom sure was messy.

I sat in the back of the van, him driving, his brother in the passenger seat and ten thousand pounds worth of cocaine in the seat beneath me. Two motorcycle cops appeared out of nowhere and pulled us over.

I thought I was going to wet myself in terror. He was all mouth and bravado, as always. I willed him to shut the fuck up but I was incapable of speaking out loud.

In the back of the Black Maria I thought of all the chances I'd had to walk away from this life. The time about 18 months ago when an old friend of mine, a decent, good man, had got back in touch when he'd heard how I was living and begged me to leave. All the looks, all the possibilities of other boyfriends over the years ... My mum, telling me I could come back home any time I wanted. And right back to the beginning, when I had first laid eyes on him in the pub. I'd known he was bad news. I was in two minds in spite of the sexual chemistry. I'm not sure I'd have gone for it had it not been for my "straight" friends looking so horrified that I was tempted to shock them. But of course, ultimately, I only had myself to blame.

And like waking from one nightmare and finding yourself in another, I opened my eyes and found that we were at the police station.

The woman on the desk was tough and expressionless as she took down my details. I had to hand over my handbag and my belt, and the laces out of my trainers. I was so scared I could barely breathe and struggled to answer all her questions.

'Are you asthmatic?' She asked.

'No. I don't think so.' Suddenly I wondered, panicking.

She looked at me for a moment and then went back to writing on the form in front of her.

Down in the bowels of the police station there was no natural light, only fluorescent strip lighting that made me feel claustrophobic and headachy. They took me to a cell and shut and locked the door behind me. I had imagined an interview room like on *The Bill*. I hadn't expected to be locked in a cell. There was a bench with a blue mattress and an open toilet. I began to shake. My lips felt dry and my nose began to run. My lip balm and tissues were in my handbag which was locked away at the desk.

I heard the sound of heavy boots, the jangling of keys and then the cell door swung open and two cops stepped in. One was older with dark brown short cropped hair flecked with grey, the other was younger, softer looking but both had that straight-backed almost military-style confidence, typical of policemen. The older one handed me a polystyrene cup of tea and smiled.

'You girls ... Didn't your mother ever tell you about keeping better company? Your boyfriend really is something. You know he's more than happy to take everyone down with him, including yourself. Now, we know *he's* bad news; we've been following him for years, just biding our time until we had enough evidence to put him away for a decent stretch. But *you*, on the other hand, you don't seem to have accrued so much as a parking ticket. Which begs the question, what's a nice girl like you doing with a scumbag like that? Now, I'm going to be absolutely straight with you: at this moment in time, you're in a lot of trouble—'

'I want to speak to a solicitor.' My knees were shaking uncontrollably and my teeth were chattering.

'You can speak to a solicitor whenever you like, Princess, but the best one on Earth isn't going to be able to keep you out of jail. We caught you, in the van, remember, sitting on a shed-load of coke. There's no arguing with evidence like that.'

'But ...' I began to cry.

'I'm here to offer you an alternative solution. One that'll keep you out of jail.'

I was crying properly now. It was hard to concentrate on what he was saying.

'Are you listening to me? I said I'm offering you a deal that'll keep you out of jail.'

He came closer to me and undid my hair from its plastic clip so that it fell around my shoulders. He ran his fingers through my hair. I was suddenly aware of my very short denim skirt, my tight white vest top that showed a good bit of boob. I took a deep breath and straightened up, and stopped crying. 'You understand, I don't make this type of offer to just anyone, do I, Barclay?'

'No, sir.' The younger cop answered.

'What it comes down to is, you be nice to us, and we'll be nice to you.' He fingered the strap of my top, slipping it casually down so that the lace of my bra was visible on one side. He stroked the lacy edge of my bra, and then stepped back, suddenly serious. 'I'm a man of my word. If you cooperate, you'll walk out of here scot-free, Princess, and that's a promise.' He stroked my cheek, which was wet with tears. 'By all means, speak to a solicitor. But the chances of him keeping you out of jail are less than zero. So, what do you say?'

I nodded, hiccoughing with tears.

He took out a pair of scissors from somewhere on his belt. I shook with fear.

'Hold still, Princess.'

He cut off my clothes, right down the middle of my bra. Everything fell in a heap at my feet. I was naked. He wolf-whistled. He put the scissors away and reached around behind me and undid the handcuffs.

And although my knees knocked together and I felt as vulnerable and as afraid as I've ever felt in my life, inside my belly was full of fire, and sent a message shooting down between my legs. Somewhere, deep in my brain, a fantasy was being fulfilled, and it was turning me on.

He looked over his shoulder.

'Give us some privacy, would you, Barclay.'

'Yes, sir.' Barclay disappeared.

'Don't worry, I'm not going to hurt you ... Don't be frightened, just relax and you'll be just fine.' He stroked my hair, my cheek. I wondered dimly what I must look like with my teary face and ruined make-up, but he didn't seem to mind. He bent down and closed his lips on mine, pushing me down onto the bench as he kissed me. His tongue was wet and slippery. He squeezed my breasts half-heartedly, as if in a hurry. Then he pushed his hand between my legs, more to open them than to touch me there. He undid his belt and grunted. He got on top of me, pressing me back into the cold mattress. He fumbled with his hand, and then he was in me. *In me.* I breathed. It was OK. I was wet for him, and again, in the back of my mind something was saying, *you wanted this, you dreamed of it*, and I pushed myself upwards towards him, embracing him like a lover.

He zipped up, leaving me wet and sticky. He sort of patted me on the shoulder, as if to say well done, or thank you, even, and then he knocked on the door and left. I heard talking outside the door. I heard radio static. The sound of footsteps in the corridor. There was a pause, and then the cell door opened again.

It was Barclay, standing before me, blushing furiously. I smiled at him. I felt yucky because of the wetness between my legs, but I felt turned on too. I'd had a taste and I wanted more.

'Hi.' I smiled at him.

'Hi.' He sat down shyly next to me. 'I haven't got long.'

'It's OK.' I took his hand. 'What do you want?'

His radio crackled. I think he took that as a sign to hurry. Looking more bashful than ever, he looked down at his lap.

'Would you?' he asked.

I smiled at him and bent over his lap, undoing his belt and zip and taking him into my mouth. He tasted of soap and water and he filled my mouth with enthusiastic thrusts of his hips. I tried to steady him, resting a hand gently on his thigh, tried to take my time and give him a decent blowjob. But he was excited and rushed, and he came within a few minutes. Afterwards he left in a hurry, as if he thought he would be interrupted at any moment.

I waited, my heart beating fast. It was like being in a dream. I wondered what would happen next – how many more would there be; would they all be so civilised? You hear some pretty scary things about police sometimes. I shivered. I heard the lock again, saw the door swing open.

'Well, well, well, what have we here then?' There were two of them. The air seemed to go cold. I straightened up, smiled, tried to look girlish – not easy while completely naked and recently ravished. The two cops were of the young gun variety, macho, loud, full of swagger, out to impress – each other, not me. In fact, it was almost as if they hardly even saw me properly at all, or maybe, that's the way they wanted to play it, anyway.

'Hey, blondie, get on the floor. On your front, that's right.'

The floor was hard concrete and so cold that it took my breath away. I heard the sound of zips being undone, of movement behind me, and then the feel of a hard, insistent cock against me, pushing inside me. I lay my cheek down against the cold floor and I closed my eyes. He was in me, and out, and in, and out. I felt him pick up his pace and urgency as he got more and more excited.

Somehow I sensed that he just wanted me like this: still and quiet and acquiescent. It suited me, to be still and to concentrate on feeling the push and drag of him entering and pulling back. Fucking without responsibilities. Or rather, being fucked without responsibilities. How else would I have ever had the chance to be so brazen, to lie on a floor and let two complete strangers fuck me?

Because he was coming, and his colleague was drawing near to take his place, and I was letting him, accepting this new cock without so much as a murmur of dissent. What woman has the freedom to behave like this normally? To live, even just for an hour or so with nothing other than sex and satisfaction as her goal and purpose; to get fucked and to satisfy men my only reason for being. For now, at least, until the world started turning again.

The second guy pulled out and shot all over my back, hitting the back of my neck, my cheek, my hair.

I lay on the concrete floor feeling the come seeping out from between my legs. And in between my legs I ached and burned and wanted, wanted so much to come. Beyond the confines of my cell I could hear shouts, alarms and the continuous slamming of doors but it felt very far away. The cell door opened again. I moved just enough to be able to see a pair of shiny leather boots enter the cell. A motorcycle cop, but I had no idea whether or not it was one of the ones who had pulled us over. I heard him stripping down, pulling down the thick leather trousers, and then I heard him kneel down behind me. He put his hands around my waist and drew me backwards onto all fours. He was so strong that I felt as light as a child being carried into bed. He wrapped one arm around my hip, his hand on my belly, holding me firmly. With his other hand he put himself into me. I gasped as he sank into me, filling me up, almost but not quite painful. I moaned; I so wanted to be fucked. I wanted it to go on forever, but he simply pushed and pushed against me and into me, faster and faster, in search only of a quick, easy relief. He emptied himself inside me, pulled out and left. I lay back down on the floor. I could feel my clit throbbing against the concrete. I needed to come, no matter what.

The door opened again, slammed shut again. Heavy footfalls came behind me and again, the sound of a zip being undone, the feel of a new, hard cock being pushed into me, harder this time, the pressure pushing me downwards and forwards so that I was rubbing against the floor. The coldness against my wet and burning pussy was a strange friction; almost painful but utterly pleasurable. I didn't care who it was who was fucking me, didn't care how many might come after, didn't care about all the noise outside the cell, the running feet, the alarms sounding. I was in a world within a world, and in that world, I was coming. He didn't take any notice or acknowledge this in any way, simply continuing until he was done, then like all the others, he knocked at the door and was let out.

Minutes passed. More minutes. I got up. I began to think that this was it – no more. I even began to feel a little bored. I certainly began to feel cold, and my clothes were lying in a destroyed heap in the corner. I picked up the remains of my vest top and wiped myself between my legs. I was still swollen and tingly there. I combed my hair with my fingers, found my hair clip on the floor and tied it back. I sat on the edge of the plastic mattress, swinging my feet. Other than that, there was nothing to do but wait.

Presently, the door opened again and Barclay came in, still looking sheepish but not blushing quite so much as before.

'Barclay!' I was as pleased to see him as if he were an old friend.

'That's Sergeant Barclay to you,' but he was smiling. 'Here, I brought you some clothes.' He handed me a neatly folded pile.

'Does that mean?'

'Yes, you're free to go. Get yourself dressed and then I'll take you out.' He turned around, rather pointlessly I thought, but it was a nice gesture and I stood up and got dressed. There was a pair of soft navy tracksuit bottoms and a white cotton T-shirt. No underwear.

'I'm sorry, that's all I could find in the stores.'

'That's OK.' The soft fabric felt warm and comforting against my skin.

I followed Barclay to the desk, feeling strangely otherworldly as I passed men who could have been there in the cell, and whom if they weren't, had probably heard about the woman who was prepared to do anything for her freedom. The woman at the desk looked me up and down and for a fraction of a second her eyebrows lifted, but then her face regained its neutral expression. I signed for my things and she handed me my bag and laces.

I roughly laced my trainers and, while my head was bent down, I thought I heard someone call out 'Blondie' and then heard something whoosh past my ear. I straightened up to see that Barclay had caught a can of coke which he handed to me. I followed him up a staircase and through several doors until at last he unlocked a door onto daylight.

'Well done. You're free to go.' Barclay said.

'Thank you.'

I stepped out into the sunshine. I walked faster and faster until I was running and I didn't stop until I had a stitch and my chest felt like it was about to burst. I leant back against a wall and cracked open the can of coke. I drank half of it in one long draught – I hadn't realised how thirsty I was. I rummaged in my bag for my lip balm and, to my great relief, I found half a pack of Marlboro lights and a lighter. I lit a cigarette and inhaled deeply. I was free.

He was sentenced to seven years in prison. Over 300 other offences were taken into consideration – I guess he wasn't the only one who wanted a clean slate. I didn't go and see him get sentenced. It was my first act of emancipation. If he could maintain good behaviour – which I doubted – he could be out in three and a half years. He wouldn't expect me to wait for him. He wasn't one of the Krays – his friends wouldn't beat up any potential new boyfriends. I could have stayed where I was and been perfectly safe, but I wanted to put geographical distance between my old life and the new one I was embarking on.

I was lucky, very lucky. Apparently I could have gone down for two years as an accessory. Instead, I walked away without so much as a caution. I felt fortunate, don't get me wrong; I had lucked out, been given a second chance. But when I thought of myself lying face down on the cold floor of that cell, hearing the door opening again and again, I couldn't help thinking that I'd *earned* it.

Night at the Museum
by Cyanne

CLAIRE SHUDDERED IN ABANDONED ecstasy, pressed between the bodies of the two security guards, their cocks filling her completely, their nylon uniforms scratching at her skin, four strong hands in her hair, holding her face, running all over her body, the cold metal of Gary's badge and stubborn plastic of his walkie-talkie and torch digging into her side. She came hard, her screams echoing around the dusty old building, silenced by Steve kissing her hard.

Claire was practically limp with pleasure and exhaustion as the guards climaxed and they collapsed in a tangle, and she giggled, remembering how only an hour ago she'd been resigned to pulling an all-nighter and by some strange chain of events she'd ended up in a cluster fuck with two rough security guards.

Earlier that evening Claire held a T'Ang Dynasty ceramic horse in her hands and her frown of concentration gave way to an appreciative smile. That flake Stuart was supposed to help her work through the night cataloguing the Treasures of the Orient exhibition before the technicians arrived first thing in the morning to lay out the gallery space, but he'd pleaded illness. A hangover most likely. But it didn't matter. She'd take the credit for the extra work and be the natural choice for the postgraduate research position at the university that was rumoured to be up for grabs in the autumn.

The museum was cold, dark and deserted, with energy-saving lights that only came on as you walked under them, leaving spooky shadowy corners. Claire looked around with a shiver. It was a bit creepy, with the dinosaur bones looming ominously in the next room, and the Chinese figures from all eras half in and out of boxes all around her. It was easy to imagine an ancient ghost skulking around something that belonged to it in a former life. She silently scolded herself for being silly.

She placed the figurine in its glass case and pulled her glasses down onto her nose, pushing the errant strands of fine blonde hair behind her ears. There had been some controversy over whether to write the labels in Classical Chinese or modern Mandarin, but, ever the perfectionist, Claire decided to do both, putting her language studies and her stunning calligraphy to good use.

The traditional sable hairbrush sailed across the cream card and Claire leaned in close to her work. Footsteps clicking up the corridor and lights snapping to life made her jump, and the brush slipped.

'Shit!'

'Sorry, didn't mean to make you jump. I'm Gary.' It was the security guard doing his rounds.

Claire blushed. She wished she didn't blush when men spoke to her, but she had always been far more at home with books and ancient relics than with living, breathing men. But that's not to say she didn't crave their touch.

'Wow, this all looks impressive.'

He strolled around the boxes, peeking inside. He had a loud voice and a jaunty swagger. A Maglite and a walkie-talkie swung from his belt.

'I know a bit of Chinese myself. Listen ... Yi, Er, San, um ... I'm stuck now. It was ages ago I learnt it. I do martial arts see. I had to learn to count in Chinese for one of the gradings.'

Claire smiled shyly and looked away. She wished she didn't have a soft spot for these rough-around-the-edges type of men. Deep down she wasn't the studious little thing everyone thought she was. Her mum was always pestering her about being almost 25, and when was she going to settle down with a nice archaeologist or something, but she liked a shaved head and tattoos. A uniform was a bonus.

Gary's security guard's uniform suited him. The navy blue jacket just hinted at muscly arms and Claire imagined they would be covered in tattoos. Her neck burned as the next wave of blush swept up to her cheeks.

'Bit shy, aren't you? You should come out with me one night, I'll show you a good time.'

'I'm just a bit busy,' Claire replied, failing to keep the smile out of her voice.

'Well, see that camera up there?' He gestured to the corner. 'You give me a wave on there when you're not busy any more and we'll have a cup of tea. How's that? And we might have to cuddle up for warmth if it gets any colder in here.'

He gave a cheeky wink and looked her up and down. Suddenly the rare artefacts didn't look so appealing. She felt like sweeping everything onto the floor and throwing herself on the table and letting him have his way with her. Images of his strong arms and solid body flashed through her mind's eye. The uncomfortable fabric of his uniform scratching her skin as he pulled her clothes off and held her close. His rough stubbly chin grazing her lips. Having to stand on tiptoe to kiss him as he was so tall. Him picking her up easily and positioning her just how he wanted her. She was bright red. He reached out and pinched her cheek.

'I could have some fun with a sweet little thing like you. Bet I'm too old for you though, aren't I?'

Not at all, she thought as she ran her eyes over his stocky frame, half obscured and half enhanced by the stiff uniform. He must be pretty strong and skilled for them to leave him in charge of all this priceless art all on his own. There was something about the badge too that aroused something in Claire. The authority, perhaps, or the fact that he was branded as a professional while he was wearing it and duty bound to behave as such.

He was looking at her, waiting for a response. Was he still joking? It was hard to tell. She stumbled over her words and he smiled at her, this time looking properly into her eyes.

'Just give me a signal on the camera if you want a bit of company, OK?'

'OK.'

She watched him walk away and felt a little flutter of excitement as he pulled on a peaked cap. He was shining his torch into secluded corners, giving her strobed glances of muscly bum cheeks in his trousers and strong tanned hands on the torch.

Claire gave herself a little shake and returned to the task in hand, but she couldn't get the thought of the strong, older man out of her head. His security guard uniform only added to his appeal, a symbol of his strength and masculinity, and such a contrast to her casual clothes and small frame.

Maybe she'd just finish these labels then wave him down for tea and see what happened. Or maybe the camera could be fun ... Maybe she could give him a little show. Her body was starting to heat up thinking about him, but her cheeks were burning at the mere thought of doing anything naughty. Her inner dialogue bantered about the ethics of giving him a flash and with every passing thought her knickers got wetter.

She started slow. She loosened her cardigan and slipped her bra off through her sleeve. Her strappy vest underneath didn't give much coverage and she let the straps fall down her shoulders so the front hung low. Walking around the other side of the table she leaned forward, pretending to be engrossed in the calligraphy but making a mess of a piece of card as the soft fabric slipped down her breasts just showing a hint of one nipple. Was he even watching? Could he see anything on the camera?

She ran her hand mock-absentmindedly over her chest, pulling the front down even more and exposing her breasts briefly. The camera made a noise and moved slightly. Was he zooming in on her?

The thought of him watching, his cock getting harder, dying to put those big hands all over her, encouraged Claire. She dropped her calligraphy brush on the floor and bent from the waist to pick it up. Her skirt was knee length but she wanted to make sure he got a glimpse of her panties so she got down on all fours to clean up the blot of ink it had left and let the skirt ride up to her waist, taking her time to give him a good look up her skirt. When she stood up, she let her skirt fall back below the knees and slipped off her cardigan, letting her top fall and showing her breasts again, before pulling it back up. The camera whirred again.

This was so much fun; she couldn't even imagine what he might do when he got his hands on her finally. Part of her just wanted to play this game all night, but part of her wanted to hear him coming down the corridor and know that she was going to get fucked.

Then came the footsteps. Her heart leapt. Would he grab her? Kiss her gently? Or was it all her, was he just being jovial?

He strode towards her. 'I've put the heating on down here. Thought you might be a bit chilly when you take everything else off.'

She blushed wildly. This was even better. He wanted her to strip on camera. As she watched him leave she rubbed her pussy lightly through her skirt. The thought of her naked and him in his full uniform, boots and hat still on, was the ultimate turn-on to her. She'd feel so vulnerable and small with a man twice her size, dressed for hard work and conflict while she was soft and naked. The image flooded her knickers.

Claire's inner slut took over. She cleared the work table

quickly. She'd have time to return to all that later. First she unzipped her skirt and, with a beautiful mixture of shyness and brazenness, let it fall to the floor, and stepped out of it. She wondered what would be sexier to take off next ... Deciding he might like to show up and take her knickers off himself, she turned her back on the camera and slid her vest top down over her hips, lingering before letting it fall. She turned around and gave him his first full view of her gorgeous small breasts, running her hands over them, imagining him gasping with desire down the corridor.

She kicked off her shoes and sat on the table, reclining slightly and opening her legs and running her hands over her body. Her skin tingled in the chilly room and her cheeks burned at the thought of him getting hard inside his uniform as he watched her on a low-res black-and-white camera.

Claire rubbed her clit lightly through the fabric of her knickers, begging him to come and get her out of them but he was making her wait. Trying desperately to coax the guard down from his office, she toyed with the sides of her underwear, like she was going to pull them down, hoping he'd come running to do it himself.

Finally it worked, and the guard appeared out of the shadows. He walked straight up to her and grabbed her roughly, kissing her hard, his rough stubble grazing her chin and his scratchy uniform harsh against her bare breasts.

He ripped her knickers away with one hand and pushed her onto the table, freeing his cock with the other hand. She arched up to meet him, desperate to have him inside her, but he held back, rubbing the tip of his cock over her swollen clit, making her moan with pleasure and frustration. The camera twisted and whirred again.

'What the fuck!' Claire jumped, futilely trying to cover herself with her cardigan. 'Is there someone up there?'

'Yeah, that's Steve. Didn't think you'd be able to handle us both, so he's just watching,' he smirked.

Claire ran through a range of emotions and landed back

at lust. Double the lust in fact.

'And is Steve dressed just like you?'

'Of course he ...' he began, then caught on to what she was saying. 'Fucking hell, girl, you're brave! Shall we get him down here then?'

Claire couldn't believe it when she heard herself say, 'Sure, why not.'

The guard beckoned into the camera, pulled away the cardigan Claire had been half covering herself with and ravished her, squeezing and biting and grazing wherever he went. Steve came down the corridor, his clothes identical to Gary, and even more rugged with tattoos down to his hands and up his neck. Claire was weak with lust, unable to do anything but moan as she was already naked, spreadeagled in a pool of her own juices as Steve walked towards her. The two men lifted her easily flat on her back on the table and she closed her eyes in pleasure and shame as Steve's hands and mouth joined Gary's all over her body. She had no idea whose finger was inside her or whose tongue was in her mouth. They were both still fully clothed, which only served to highlight her nakedness.

Steve pulled Claire to her feet and she fell against him dizzily. Gary had produced a bottle of something from God knows where and was drizzling her in some kind of oil or lube. He rubbed her back hard and trickled more down her front over her tits and Steve rubbed it into her nipples, while Gary ran his hand between her arse cheeks. The culmination of sensations was getting too much and she swayed on her feet, but they held her easily.

Gary's finger was probing her arse and Steve's kiss silenced her automatic protests, letting her settle into enjoying his finger sliding easily in and out. Her pussy ached for attention but got none yet.

Steve held her as Gary sat on the table, his cock springing up eagerly through his open flies but his eyes slightly obscured by his hat. Steve lifted her easily and lowered her down as Gary guided his cock into her arse, taking hold of her waist and thrusting gently.

Claire shuddered as the two men lifted her up and down Gary's cock, supporting her weight so all she could feel was him sliding in and out. Gary gripped her waist as Steve got down on his knees and kissed and licked his way from her feet up to her inner thighs. She tried to push her pussy towards his face but Gary held her tight, pushing further into her.

'What do you reckon, Gary?' Steve grinned up at them, 'I think she wants me to eat her pussy, reckon we should make her wait a bit longer?'

Gary lifted her so just the tip of his cock was inside her arse and bounced her gently so it teased around the entrance. Claire was moaning and thrashing around, loving the tease yet desperate to have the full pressure.

'I don't know, I think she is used to getting what she wants, I think you should make her wait a bit longer,' Gary said, 'either that or make her beg for it.'

Steve licked the tip of her clit and she cried out.

'Oh she definitely wants it. Say please.'

Claire mumbled and struggled.

'Say you want me to lick your pussy, and say please.'

'Please ...' Claire muttered.

'Please what?'

Even poised on the brink of orgasm with her pussy right in Steve's face and Gary's cock inside her Claire faltered over the words.

'Please lick my pussy!'

Gary groaned and pulled her down again, and Steve took his hat off and leaned into her, kissing gently at first then licking lightly. Claire melted into the sensation of a rock hard cock up her arse and a tongue on her clit. She came hard, bucking against Steve's face. Her pussy was begging to be fucked and like a mind-reader Steve pressed one finger inside her, bringing on another wave of orgasm.

He stood up and freed his cock, motioning to Gary to tilt her backward. He rolled on a rubber and slid into her, their cocks almost colliding inside her, and began to move slowly at first, then harder as she loosened up to the unusual but delicious feeling of having both her holes filled. Her legs were pulled into a wide V, her juices staining their uniforms and her head thrown back in abandon as her final orgasm ripped through her body. She lay there pressed between them as they grunted to their climaxes and they all collapsed breathless on the table.

Steve picked up his abandoned hat and stuck it on Claire's head as she laid there naked willing her eyesight and heart rate to return to normal.

'You can keep that as a souvenir', he said, and they all laughed.

Clean-up on Aisle Five
by Elizabeth Coldwell

HALF A HEAD OF lettuce and a carton of sour milk. Justin didn't even need to check the fridge to know those were the only things waiting for him on his return from business in New York. All the way back on the flight from La Guardia he had been making a mental list of the groceries he would need to pop out and buy when he finally got home: half-a-dozen eggs, streaky bacon, a large white loaf ... Though in truth, the larder could have been fully stocked and he would still have been itching to dump his bags and dash straight over to the all-night supermarket. Throughout a long week of tedious high-level meetings and thoroughly forgettable business lunches, he had been sustaining himself with thoughts of Janice, with her dirty-blonde hair and her plump, pink-painted lips, and now he was desperate to see his favourite checkout girl again.

More accurately, he was desperate to see her in her uniform again. Like many men, for as long as he could remember, he'd had a thing about girls in uniform. But not for him the predictable allure of the naughty nurse, with her starched white cap and saucy stockings hiding beneath her outwardly respectable dress, or the adult schoolgirl, all pigtails, pout and teeny-tiny skirt. No, the outfit which had always made Justin's heart beat faster and the blood begin to rush to his cock was the cheap nylon overall worn by checkout girls and fast-food restaurant staff. No matter how gaudy the colouring or unflattering the fit, those overalls never failed to turn him on. He had no idea why. Nothing he could remember from his formative years could have prompted such unorthodox desires; his mother – according to the therapists the usual source of a man's deepest fetish – had been a highly successful barrister, for goodness sake. If the theories were correct, he should have been fantasising about women in powdered wigs and long black gowns. Instead, even as he stowed his suitcase in the hall of his second-floor flat and reached for the carrier bags which hung on the back of the front door, the ones which earned him extra loyalty points whenever he used them, he was already growing excited at the thought of seeing Janice in her deeply unattractive but oh-so-sexy attire.

It was gone one in the morning by now, but as far as Justin was concerned, that was the perfect time to shop. In the small hours of a midweek morning, the supermarket would be populated only by insomniacs, shift workers and possibly the odd clubber who had come in to feed the chocolate cravings caused by a sudden attack of the munchies. Surely no one else would be there primarily to gaze on Janice, the nylon-clad goddess of the checkouts.

Tonight, he decided, would be the night when he finally asked her out. He had tried on a number of previous occasions, but always lost his nerve at the last moment. Not that there was anything stopping her from accepting, as far as he knew. In all the months he'd been shopping here, he had never noticed a ring on her finger, or overheard her chatting about children or some dull domestic issue, as the other women who manned the tills did. Fat, 40-something Mary, who was usually stationed on the counter with the cigarettes and the lottery terminal, was always moaning about what her idle lump of a husband had or hadn't done that day. And then there was Sanjeeta, fretting about whether the oldest of her three sons would get the grades he needed in his exams to enable him to study medicine. Janice, though – Janice was untouched by such distractions, as far as Justin could tell. She sat serenely at her register, scanning each item in turn, while the poppers on the front of her pale yellow overall strained just enough to offer him a tantalising glimpse of the lacy bra she wore beneath it.

Oh, to peel her out of that overall, he thought, and discover the delicious beauty of the body beneath it. He was standing at the bakery counter, crusty bloomer in hand, so lost in his erotic reverie that he didn't at first comprehend the significance of the sight before him. Leaning over what appeared to be a broken freezer unit, hauling out packets of fish fingers before they thawed and were ruined, was a young woman. A young woman whose blondish hair, twisted into a knot on the back of her head and held in place with a white scrunchie and a number of Kirby grips, was immediately familiar.

He wasn't sure whether he had ever seen Janice from the waist down, but now he revelled in the view. Her overall was stretched tautly over her big bottom; a bottom whose cheeks he yearned to squeeze as he deftly eased his cock between them. The hem had ridden up as she bent to empty the freezer, allowing him a good look at her luscious, plump thighs. There was no one else around: no shoppers browsing in the immediate aisles; no staff standing behind the bakery or deli counters. It would have taken a much stronger man than Justin to resist the temptation Janice's provocative position presented. Aware that he was running the risk of being banned from every branch of Val-u-save in the country, Justin dropped his shopping basket to the floor and grabbed the startled girl around the waist.

He just had time to register the feel of soft, womanly flesh beneath slightly scratchy nylon before she started to slap his hands away.

'What the hell do you think you're doing?' she hissed.

He breathed in the scent of her: cheap musk body spray; fresh sweat and whatever fabric conditioner she used on her overall. Heaven, he thought. 'God, Janice, you're gorgeous,' he murmured. 'I've wanted you for so long, and just the sight of you with your luscious bum trying to burst out of your lovely, lovely overall ...' Justin hoped he was conveying something of the lust Janice never failed to arouse in him, but he suspected all he was doing was earning himself a slap round the chops.

For a moment, Janice stopped wriggling in his arms, and then she started moving again, but this time with a different purpose. It wasn't difficult for Justin to realise why. Though he was only a little over average in height, and had rather too beaky a nose to be considered conventionally handsome, he was blessed with a very big cock. That cock had begun to thicken and swell as soon as he had caught sight of Janice and now, pressed against her ample bum cheeks, it was almost fully erect. She ground herself against him, driving him almost delirious with the need to fuck her.

Her small hand reached between their two bodies, seeking for the zip of his fly and tugging it down. Now it was his turn to protest. Much as part of him – the part which was currently grasped in Janice's warm, teasing fingers – wanted to fuck her right there, over the freezer in the middle of the store, he knew that was just too risky.

'What if someone catches us?' he asked, his voice almost cracking with the strain of being expertly wanked by Janice. He couldn't believe how rapidly her mood had changed from reluctant to rampant, but he supposed that having your hands on almost eight inches of fat, veiny cock-flesh could do that to a woman.

'OK,' she said, pausing in her movements for a moment. 'Follow me.'

He did as she asked, praying that no one spotted them and realised that his cock was poking blatantly out of his fly, plum-red and glistening and more than ready to bury itself in Janice's soft, willing body. Swiftly, Janice led him through a thick plastic slatted curtain into a storage area. It was where the trolleys for moving stock round the aisles were kept, and was littered with cardboard boxes and signs for some forthcoming in-store promotion. The place was chilly and smelled vaguely of disinfectant, but at least they were away from the main shop floor. After taking a quick glance around to make sure they were completely alone, Janice unfastened Justin's trousers and yanked them down to the floor. She took hold of his erection once more, and picked up where she had left off, stroking it and rubbing it between her palms with a look of greedy anticipation on her face.

Suddenly, she broke off and began to undress. She popped open the fasteners of the overall and made to shrug it off her shoulders, but Justin stopped her. 'Leave it on,' he begged. 'Please, leave it on.'

She did as he asked, letting the garment flap loose as she reached to push her knickers down and off. Afterwards, Justin couldn't have said what colour those knickers were, or whether they were plain cotton or fancy lace. His attention was purely on the way her skin looked against the yellow of the overall, pale and slightly freckly. She didn't bother to remove her bra, but in Justin's eyes that simply made her look more sexy, more magnificently slutty; half-dressed and eager for his meat.

She squatted down on her haunches, reached for his cock and tugged the long foreskin back and forth a couple of times before taking the shiny, wet head in her mouth. Justin stifled a groan as she sucked him, not half as confident as Janice seemed to be that they would remain undisturbed. Though as her tongue lapped over his helmet with slow, languid strokes, he began to forget about the possibility of discovery. Somewhere in the far distance he could hear a Tannoy announcement, but the words were meaningless; his world had shrunk to the immediate confines of the storage area, and all that mattered was that Janice kept on easing his cock as far as she could between her lips.

Justin was completely lost in the pleasure of the moment when she decided to stop what she was doing. He begged her to swallow his cock once more, but in response she bent over a nearby trolley, offering her rump to him. This time, the overall was raised so high that it failed to cover her arse, and he was able to feast his gaze on the plump lips of her sex where they peeked out seductively from the apex of her thighs. For the second time in ten minutes, temptation got the better of him: he lined his cock up and, with one hard thrust, parted those lips and pushed up into the velvety recesses of her cunt. She was tight, and he was huge, and at first it was a slightly snugger fit than he would have liked if he wasn't going to spill his spunk within a couple of strokes. But gradually she began to relax and open up, letting him go deeper and deeper. She clung on to the trolley's handle, giving little squeals of delight and urging him to fuck her harder. He barely needed any encouragement: as his groin slapped against Janice's buttocks and he felt the stimulation of her regulation overall against his overheated skin, he realised he was experiencing the most profound pleasure sex had ever given him. His uniform fetish was being fulfilled in the most delightful way possible and he never wanted the moment to end. But as Janice rubbed her own clit until the muscles of her pussy spasmed in orgasm around him, it was all too much. Justin groaned, pulled out of her tightly clinging cunt and shot great gouts of spunk all over her bare bum cheeks.

'That was fucking amazing,' he sighed, flopping back against the wall.

Janice reached for her discarded knickers and stepped into them. She gave him an affectionate kiss, fondling his spent cock as she did. 'I'm due my break in ten minutes,' she said as she fastened her overall. 'Go pay for your shopping and I'll see you in the car park.'

Don't tell me you're ready to go again? Justin thought, even as his cock began to stir at the thought of fucking his uniform-clad sweetheart.

Fully dressed once more, he made his way out to where

he had left his basket of groceries. He noticed that Janice was by the broken freezer, deep in conversation with another of the checkout assistants, a pretty black girl of around 20 who he didn't recognise. She fills that uniform out nicely, was Justin's immediate thought. The girl looked wide-eyed at whatever Janice was saying, then stared at Justin – or, more accurately, at Justin's bulging crotch – and giggled.

'This is Nancy,' Janice whispered, as Justin passed them. 'I hope you like her, because in a few minutes she's going to help me introduce you to a very special two-for-one offer ...'

Nights in Black Satin
by Sophia Valenti

I TOOK A SIP of red wine, savouring the liquor's lush flavour as I reclined on the sofa and watched Brenda scurry across the living room. The lace-trimmed bodice of her French maid's uniform hugged her torso like a second skin – her body's contours accentuated by the snug-fitting corset she wore beneath it – and her ruffled skirt bounced as she trotted across the living room in her five-inch patent-leather heels. As she bent over to stroke her hot-pink feather duster across the wooden coffee table, I admired her toned legs encased in sheer silk stockings, the seams of which were perfectly straight. I knew she was bending over so deeply for my benefit, and I appreciated the lovely view of her panties stretched tightly across her bottom.

Brenda is the quintessential lady's maid: beautiful, indulgent and completely subservient. And every weekend, she's all mine. During the week, however, when Brenda leaves my home and heads back into the business world, she leaves her sissy self behind and once again becomes Brett, my handsome stockbroker boyfriend. I love both sides of Brett's personality, knowing that I can call on him to be my picture-perfect escort for corporate social events, yet have a sexy housemaid at my beck and call on the weekends. For me, it's the best of both worlds – and from the massive hard-on that I see stretching his pretty panties every time we play these dress-up games, I can tell that he enjoys our playtime as much as I do.

Brett's transformation began with a late-night whispered confession. Early in our relationship, he revealed that he loved the feeling of satin cupping his cock and balls – and then went further and told me he had his own stash of panties at home that he sometimes wore underneath his custom-made suits. Making that admission during a post-tryst cuddle made his dick swell rapidly, despite the fact that he'd had a body-shaking orgasm mere minutes before. The idea of my man in frilly lingerie didn't turn me on – at first. But seeing his reaction to simply talking about panties made me eager to explore his kink. Flashing him a wicked smile, I climbed out of bed to rummage around in my lingerie drawer. I'd ordered a pair of sleek French-cut undies months ago online and had been disappointed that they'd been too big for me. I'd shoved them in my stash, and they were immediately forgotten. But at that moment, I was as pleased as punch that I hadn't tossed them in the trash.

Brett's eyes grew wide as I approached him, holding the feminine undergarment in my hands. I didn't say a word as I slipped the panties over his feet and up his legs; my intent was obvious. He didn't speak either but kept his eyes locked on the bunched-up satin as I tugged it upward. Once I'd worked the panties up to his muscular thighs, he lifted his ass off the bed to help me settle the undies around his hips. They were incredibly snug, but the sight of his dick rapidly hardening beneath the satin made my mouth water. I leaned down and ran my tongue along his shaft, wetting the white fabric and making it almost translucent with my saliva. Brett tangled his fingers in my hair as I teased his slick cock with my lips, making it swell until the head poked up out of the elastic waistband. A pearly drop of pre-come was perched on the tip of his dick, and I swiped it up with my tongue before sucking and tickling his cockhead and stroking his satiny bulge. Brett came in no time, clutching my hair and groaning as he climaxed. His sticky semen splashed against his washboard abs as I continued to tickle his sensitive balls through the filmy panties.

After that night, I was hooked. I began regularly buying lingerie for Brett: lace-trimmed slips, delicate bras, and panties in a rainbow of colours. I also began insisting he wear his presents whenever we were alone on the weekends. Seeing how turned on he became when wearing women's clothes started to turn me on too. And I'll confess that I soon preferred seeing him in girlie undies. In addition to my growing appreciation of his fetish, I also noticed a distinct transformation in his personality when he was dressed in frilly things. When he donned satin or silk, his usual gregariousness disappeared, and he acted more coquettish and coy – almost like a girl. I found it rather charming, and his subservient behaviour seemed to trip some sort of erotic wire inside me. I gradually grew more aggressive when we played our dress-up games, telling him how and where we'd have sex. Eventually, I stopped telling him, and I'd simply take control of the action, pulling his panties down and leaving them banded around his thighs as I'd climb on top of his dick, pin his wrists above his head, and ride him until we'd each reached a thrilling climax.

I was having the best sex of my life, and it never occurred to me that it could get even better. But a few weeks into our lingerie-fuelled adventures, I saw something in a store window that would change everything. I was strolling through a high-end shopping district in the city, looking for shoes, when I passed an erotic boutique and did a double-take. The window display was elegant and intriguing, featuring a selection of handcrafted whips and Victorian-style hairbrushes, but what really caught my eye was the outfit on the mannequin: a black satin French maid's outfit. It was a perky off-the-shoulder frock, trimmed with white lace, its short, poufy skirt supported by layers of frilly crinolines. The sight of it made my heart race and my pussy moisten. I had to have it, and more importantly, I had to see Brett in it.

Inside the store, the atmosphere and the staff were warm and welcoming. I didn't hesitate to reveal to the salesgirl that I was shopping for my boyfriend. She didn't even blink, and the way she so readily produced a Brett-sized dress from the back room told me that I was not the first woman to enter her shop who wanted to sissify her man. With her guidance, I was soon fully equipped with all of the naughty accessories I would need to turn Brett into Brenda – my own personal French maid.

I called Brett as soon as I returned home, telling him that I'd have a sensual surprise waiting for him at my place that evening and he shouldn't be late. He pressed me for answers, but I revealed nothing. It wasn't as hard as it sounds. My mind was filled with a never-ending stream of obscene images, which nearly monopolized all of my thought power. Although I'm fairly certain he mistook my reticence as an aloof tease. No matter, I was more than willing to let him draw his own conclusions – especially since it was to my benefit.

As I awaited Brett's arrival, I dressed with care, donning carefully pressed tuxedo pants, a crisp white shirt and black suspenders. From the neck down, I may have looked like a man, but from the shoulders up, I was all woman, with slicked-back blonde hair, smoke-grey shadowed eyes and blood-red lipstick.

I could barely contain my excitement. Every time I tried to take my mind off my sinful plan, my dirty thoughts immediately returned to images of Brett clad in that black satin uniform. I felt the moisture seeping from between my pussy lips. I knew with one flick of my fingertip I'd be able to send myself over the edge, but I've always felt that anticipation made our games that much sweeter – and I knew that this night had the potential to be the sweetest yet.

Brett rang my bell at nine o'clock – right on time. The promise of a kink-filled evening was apparently too thrilling for him to resist. When I opened the door, he tried to kiss me, but I put my hand on his chest to stop him and then pushed him away from me.

'That's a rather forward way to greet your employer,' I said sharply. His shock and confusion registered immediately on his face.

'Employer? Jessie, I–' I silenced him by placing one neatly manicured finger on his lips.

'That's better. Now, follow me. You need to be properly dressed for your orientation.'

Brett's discombobulated look amused me so much that I could barely stay in character. I managed, though, because thoughts of what he was going to wear – and what I was going to do after that – had me breathlessly hot.

I motioned for Brett to follow me and headed to my bedroom. Once I crossed the threshold, I stepped aside so he could see the French maid uniform I'd laid out on the bed. His eyes grew wide as he took in the sight of the frilly outfit, thigh-high fishnet stockings, shiny patent leather pumps and a selection of dainty underthings meant to enhance Brenda's feminine silhouette.

'You are to change immediately, and then come out to see me in the parlour. And do something with that hair and face of yours. I'll not take the chance of having an impromptu guest greeted by a slovenly servant.' At the mention of a guest, Brett stood up straight and I could sense his fear. But even as the panic rose in his face, I saw the telltale bulge of his rock-hard dick tenting his slacks. 'No, no one will be visiting us tonight, but you need to be diligent in keeping up your appearance if you want to be a part of my household.'

I turned dismissively and stomped out of the room, resisting the urge to look back. I so loved toying with him, but I had a very specific agenda for the night and wanted everything to go as planned. Besides, Brett had plenty of practice dressing and making up his own face. He didn't need my help, which would only muddy the waters of our new arrangement. I wanted to maintain my dominant position, to keep him on edge – and to keep his questions unanswered for as long as possible. Keeping him off kilter would add to his arousal. Not knowing what would happen next would ensure that his cock would be throbbing and aching for release.

Back in the living room, I leaned back on the couch and rested my lace-up Oxfords on the coffee table. I heard the halting click-clack of unsteady feet in high heels coming from the hallway and turned to see my beautiful Brenda clad in black satin and white lace. My breath caught in my throat at the sight of her. The dress fit her like a glove, snug around her chest and nipped in at her waist, thanks to the cincher that I'd thoughtfully supplied. I bit my lip, knowing that Brenda's frilly skirts must be hiding a stiff cock. The height of her heels significantly altered her posture and helped highlight the muscular definition of her fishnet-clad calves. I'd never seen my girl look more delectable.

'Well done, Brenda. Your face and hair are impeccable.' I wasn't lying. Her long black hair was slicked back into a neat bun, with not a flyaway in sight, and her face was elegantly made up, with just a hint of brown eye shadow and rose-coloured blush. But at that moment, I only had eyes for her bright red lips, so glossy and irresistible.

I beckoned her toward me, and she slowly tottered closer. While Brenda loves ladies shoes, the four-inch heels I'd chosen for her that first night were the highest she'd worn to date. I enjoyed the sight of her struggling to walk as gracefully as possible.

Brenda's eyes were slightly lowered, and although she was taller than me, I felt ten feet tall as I stood before my meek maid. 'I think we're ready to begin your orientation,' I announced, taking her chin in my hand and running my thumb beneath her pouty bottom lip. I could swear that it seemed to quiver, which sent a charge through me. 'I have very specific requirements for this position, Brenda. Are you willing to do whatever it takes to keep me happy?'

'Yes ... yes, ma'am,' Brenda answered, nervously fluttering her eyelashes. Hearing her voice, so agreeable and compliant, encouraged me to continue.

'Good, then we have an understanding,' I replied, my voice coming in a raspy whisper. I ran a hand back across Brenda's hair, thinking that on my next trip to the boutique I'd have to pick up a lace-trimmed cap to top off her look.

I rested my hands on Brenda's shoulders and stared into her eyes for a moment, seeing the fear warring with desire and knowing that the man inside these frilly feminine trappings was getting as much of a charge out of this scene as I was – and he didn't even know what else I had up my sleeve, or should I say, in my pants.

'On your knees,' I demanded, pressing on Brenda's shoulders to ensure she didn't delay in following my order.

Brenda sank down before me, her crinolines rustling noisily as she shifted. She looked upward with a worshipful gaze that thrilled me to the core. Keeping my eyes locked on hers, I slowly lowered my zipper and fished out the strap-on dildo that I had hidden beneath my slacks.

'You know what to do,' I said, my voice hoarse with want. Brenda's eyes reflected her shock and hesitation. She haltingly parted her lips and cautiously brought her head forward. Impatient, I grabbed hold of her perfectly tucked bun, and with one rough tug, the length of my dick disappeared down her throat. After a small cough, she managed to swallow all six inches of silicone, her nose brushing against the teeth of my open zipper. She pulled back to take a breath, and I admired the streaks of her glossy lipstick smeared along my shaft in the moment before she dove back down, enveloping my tool a second time

'That's better,' I cooed. 'If you want to be my maid, you'll need to give me the best blowjob you've ever delivered. And that's saying something for a slut like you.'

My nasty talk seemed to spur Brenda on, and she began

bobbing her head up and down my cock at a furious pace, almost as if she had something to prove. The sight of her kneeling before me in her uniform and the sound of her satin and crinolines whispering with her every movement made my pussy drip. Having my boyfriend dressed as my own personal servant girl while he sucked my strap-on dick felt deliciously dirty. As much as I enjoyed it, however, it was time to move on to my next surprise.

Brenda was still slobbering over my dick like a woman possessed, but I grabbed hold of her hair – which was beginning to escape its tightly tucked updo – and yanked her head back.

'Nice work,' I said, gesturing toward the flesh-coloured toy, which was slick with saliva. 'You'll be glad in a minute that you made it so wet.' I tugged on the back of her dress, yanking her upward, and dragged her – slightly stumbling in her heels – over to the sofa, and then tossed her over the arm of it. I gathered up her skirts, piling up the frilly fabric on the small of her back. Her satin-clad ass was the best thing I'd seen all day; I yanked down her panties, leaving them banded around her thighs, and dragged two spit-slick fingers between her cheeks. When I grazed her asshole, Brenda moaned; it was a sound filled with hunger and longing, and I didn't hesitate to work one, and then two fingers into her eager opening. When I felt she'd been properly stretched, I placed the shiny head of my cock at her backdoor.

I rested my dick there, teasing her with the promise of penetration as I reached into my pocket for a small bottle of lube that I flicked open with my thumb. I drizzled some of the slick liquid along the length of my dick before pushing the faux cock slowly but steadily into her snug passage. Brenda moaned steadily and rhythmically as I pumped my shaft in and out of her hole. The base of the toy was rocking up against me, pushing me further toward orgasm with each delicious thrust. I rested one hand on the top of her stocking, and then reached down to tickle her thigh through the holes in her fishnets. I scratched and teased her flesh as I continued to pump my hips. My other hand gradually wandered up to stroke Brenda's satin-clad chest, pinching her nipples in turn through the slippery fabric of the bodice. The sight of my beautiful boyfriend submitting to me so willingly, the sensation of all of that luxurious fabric under my hands and the delicious friction of the toy against my clit all combined to push me over the edge.

I was lost in the haze of a delirious orgasm as I ground my hips against Brenda's firm bottom cheeks. When I finally caught my breath, I reached underneath Brenda, searching under her petticoats for her hot, hard cock. I wrapped my fingers around her shaft, stroking her firmly while still keeping my dick lodged in her ass.

'Such a sweet little maid,' I whispered in her ear. 'We're going to have so much fun together, you and I.'

Brenda merely groaned in response, thrusting backward to impale herself even more on the toy and then bucking forward to fuck my fist. She jerked back and forth, working for her release. I let her take control – and take her pleasure from me; she'd more than earned it. Our role-play had gotten her so hot, it didn't take long for Brenda's dick to pulse in my hand, her cockhead grinding against the scratchy nylon netting of her crinolines as she moaned and reached her peak.

I gently pulled my cock from her spasming asshole, stroking her dishevelled hair away from her sweaty face. 'Looks like your first chore for tonight will be doing the laundry,' I whispered in her ear.

'As you wish,' Brenda answered, turning toward me, her eyes shining. Our gloss-slick lips met in a moment of slippery, perfumed pleasure – the most sensual lip lock that I'd ever experienced. And with that kiss, we sealed our kinky little pact.

Our arrangement might not be conventional, but it works for us, with just the right proportions of give and take.

Brenda's sexy subservience and my newfound dominance are two halves of a perfect pair, and together we make each other whole.

Exemplary Employee
by Charlotte Stein

HE ALWAYS COMES TO my house wearing a sort of tunic, pristine and white and pinned at one shoulder. Like a doctor, from the future. His trousers usually match, too, and so do his little white shoes.

He should look prim or weird, I know, but he never does. He looks like a professional, with his fine blond hair brushed down smooth and flat. And his little case, filled with professional things like oils and lotions and exfoliating mitts.

They are the kind of things that any masseuse would wear, or carry around. And he has the kind of accent best suited to masseuses – an accent you expect. Sort of Swedish or maybe Norwegian, with few correct English words in between it all.

I think he's memorised the right phrases to say, when he visits a client. *Would you like to lie down now*, that sort of thing. *Shall I put on the music? Do you want the jasmine? Soft, or hard?*

Though he usually doesn't ask now. He knows what I like, and what I don't like. He's very good – very business-like and utterly thorough. All of his clients speak very highly of him, and I can see why. Who wouldn't want a tall, blond, handsome Swedish man coming to rub his hands over their bare bodies, twice a week?

It used to be once, but I've upped it since then. Now that I know that he's so well trained, and careful, and diligent. I mean – just look at that pristine white. He is obviously excellent at his job. His natural manner seems to be one of utter calm and steadiness, which is a perfect match, really, for this kind of work.

'Would you like to remove your clothes?' he says, and I do. I used to pop into the bathroom and come out in a towel, when he first started coming. But now I don't see the need, I really don't. He obviously divorces himself very successfully from his work – why, I might as well be getting a massage from a robot.

A tall, handsome robot, who last week said to me: 'No, no girlfriend', when I asked him if he had one. So I had said: 'Boyfriend, then?' But he had simply laughed, and replied, 'Girls. I like girls.' And then, after a moment, the strangest thing: 'You have excellent buttocks, Miss Hartford.'

Which is something I'd never really thought about, before. I suppose it might be because he generally massages a lot of older ladies, and perhaps my bottom seems a bit firmer in comparison. Though then again my breasts aren't quite as perky as they could be, but he still tells me that they're excellent too.

So maybe he just says it to everyone, to make them feel better.

'Can I massage the breasts?' he asks, which seems odd. Because usually, he doesn't ask at all. I mean, it's part of an all-over-body massage, isn't it? What would be the point, if he missed out a large area on my chest?

'Of course,' I tell him, and he slides oil-slick fingers over my nipples, in firm decisive strokes.

I must confess, I get a little tingle, when he does it. I've had them before, of course, because he's very good at his job and sometimes the whole thing leaves me quite breathless. But this seems like a little bit more than in previous sessions, and it could be because every time he squeezes my breasts in his large hands, he finishes on a slight tug of my nipples – which are erect by this point, naturally.

'Very good,' he says, and I wonder what he means. It's hard to tell, because he has such an impassive face. Such serene blue eyes – and oh, that delightful little cleft in his chin. Though if he were ugly, I'm sure the whole thing would be just as nice. It's lovely to have a bit of human contact, you know.

'Turn over now,' he says, which is a little disappointing. It was making me feel quite flushed, all that massaging of my breasts. If it had gone on a little longer, I don't think I would have complained.

'Shhh,' he says. 'Don't worry, don't worry.'

Though I can't say why. Do I seem worried? I'm not in the least bit concerned, in his capable, professional hands.

Though when I glance to the left, I notice he's unbuttoned that strange clasp, which holds his uniform closed at his left shoulder. I mean, it's not gaping open, or anything. And I can't really say much – perhaps it just came undone on its own, or maybe he was feeling a little hot. But still ... it's odd.

And it's odd when he says *mmmm* too, as his hands glide up and down my back. Odd and entirely pleasant – he *really* knows what he's doing.

I squirm, when I feel him drizzle more oil all over me. Now I'm practically sopping, when he starts rubbing me again. So it's not really a surprise, when his hand accidentally slides right over the hills of my buttocks, and all the way in between.

I don't say anything, however. He's such a professional that he's probably mortified, to find that his slippery fingers are between the cheeks of my bottom. Either that, or this is just a new part of the massage – which I think it could well be. I mean, what's an all-over-body massage, if it avoids a great big giant place like ... there?

He clearly knows what he's doing.

'You like me to stop?' he asks – see what I mean about

his politeness? Just so charming.

'Of course not,' I reply. 'You do what you think is best, Sven.'

I don't think his real name is Sven. But I've never said anything, and see no reason to mention it now.

'Very good,' he says, and he sounds a bit breathless, poor thing. It must be the heat in here – it's positively scorching.

So I tell him to take some of his uniform off. You know, just to alleviate matters. But oh dear me, he goes for the top half first and I can't think what to say to that, apart from the little chuckle that comes out of me. Oh dear me no, he can't take the top off – that's the part of his uniform that marks him out as a diligent professional.

No, it has to be the trousers. Just the trousers, and maybe the shoes too.

Now he's just in his underpants and his white tunic, sliding his hand back and forth between my legs. He gently parts them so that he can work freely and easily, and tells me that he's going to use a soothing, scent-free oil for the best results.

Though in all honesty, I can't see why he needs it there. I seem to be quite well lubricated already, and one of his long, thick fingers slides into my sex no problems at all. He's breathing fairly hard and high now, which I suppose is to be expected. I mean, it must be hard work to have to reach a little way under someone's body, like this, in order to get at their clit. And he has his thumb in my pussy while he goes about it, so I can't imagine it's easy.

'You like?' he asks. 'You like?'

And at the very least, he deserves a yes. Even when he slides one finger of his free hand between my buttocks, again, and passes it over my arsehole – he still deserves a yes. After all, it's not unpleasant. Not even when he pushes it in a little way, and fingers me there while he strokes my pussy.

'So good,' he moans, because I am, you know. I'm a very good client, indeed. I give myself over to all these soaring, jostling tingles the minute he tells me I should, though whether he intended to order me to *come now, come now*, I'm not entirely sure.

His English just isn't very good at all.

When he comes again the next day – I asked him for an extra appointment, and considering my generous tip he was only too happy to oblige – we get right down to business. But this time, I ask him if I might lie on my back. I explain that I thoroughly enjoyed the breast massage, and a little ghost of a smile plays on his pale lips.

There's nothing wrong with taking pride in your work, I want to tell him, but instead I just strip out of my clothes and lie down on the bed.

He gets straight to work – of course he does. Slicking his hands with oil, drizzling it over my tight nipples and my freshly waxed mound. He's an artist, really.

'You feel nice and relaxed now?' he asks, and I give him what he clearly wants. I tell him that he did an excellent job yesterday, and that I was thrilled with the results.

At which he smiles again, and begins easing all that oil over my waiting body. Slow strokes, at first, but then longer. And longer. From the hollow of my throat, to the jut of my hips and down, all the way down. I must say I'm quite ticklish, in the foot area, so when he gets there, of course I laugh.

His expression is quite startled and odd, when the little sound escapes from me. Almost hurt, I think, and then it occurs to me – why, he just wants to be sure he's doing a good job. What sort of person likes having someone laugh at them, while they're in the middle of such a delicate operation?

So I explain – I'm just ticklish, there. At which he relaxes once more. He relaxes so much that he takes his trousers off again, and it doesn't escape my notice that he's wearing different underpants. These ones are quite small and almost transparent – what Americans might call tighty-whities, I suppose – and they reveal a lot.

It makes me want to avert my eyes, but when you really think about it, that would be impossibly rude. There he is, complimenting my body and rubbing oil all over me, and I'm not showing the slightest bit of appreciation for his.

So I stare, at the distinct shape of his erect cock, through the thin material.

Of course I'm not the least bit offended. By it being erect, I mean. I suppose other women might be, but I find it as flattering as I'm sure he intends it. Plus I have to feel some measure of sympathy for the poor fellow. He clearly has a large appendage. It must be terribly difficult to hide any arousal, while massaging supple young bodies.

And especially when he has his hands between my legs again, and is rubbing my slit gently, up and down, up and down.

'Yes, very nice,' he says, and I feel so obliged to tell him the same. Thankfully, however – being the well-trained masseuse that he is – he does it for me.

'You like this,' he says, and touches the angular shape in his underwear. 'You like it, good. Watch it while I massage.'

I wonder if he intends it as some sort of meditation or concentration technique. You know – focusing on one single point in order to drain out the body's impurities, and the like. And he's right, because I can feel my body's impurities draining out of me right now. He has two fingers in my pussy and he's rubbing my clit with the heel of his palm and I'm shivering all over, like a mad thing.

'That's it,' he says. 'Let it go, let it all go.'

And I tingle just like I did yesterday – at his behest, with his large, strong hands between my legs.

However, this time is different. This time, he does not

begin to pack up, once his hands are off me, and away. Instead, he continues to kneel by my liquid body, breathing hard. He tells me over and over, *very good*, and then finally, after a while, says something he's never said before.

Though I suppose all of these are new techniques and explorations, so it seems rather pointless to halt proceedings now.

'Oh, I am very stressful,' he says, poor chap. Then, almost haltingly and with his eyes sort of sliding away from me: 'Would you help me with the stressfulness?'

And I think to myself: well. What sort of decent-minded Christian woman would refuse? Hasn't he been utterly considerate and attentive to my needs? Professional in all respects? Of course he has.

I would only be too happy to relieve any stress he has, and I tell him so immediately.

He smiles – almost bashfully, I think – shortly before I ask him if he'd like to take his tunic off. I mean, I'd prefer for him to keep it on. But if the tension is all in his shoulders, then I'll have to work there.

But he shakes his head, and explains further for me, patiently. I'm so glad he's patient, because of course I have no experience with this sort of thing. He is the masseuse, and he's going to have to guide me if he wants a successful relieving of his stress.

'No, no. It is in this area,' he says, and points to his groin.

Oh, what a dafty I am! I should have *known*. Clearly he is in dire need of stress relief, in that particular area. As my husband would have said, were he still about: *good one, Margot! Gone and cocked it, yet again!*

Which I suppose is a rather appropriate term, given the circumstances. *Cocked it*.

Sven tugs those little underpants down, and I sit up, ready to set to work. I crack my knuckles – you know, just to get everything nice and limber – and then await instructions. I'm sure he's going to give me instructions – and the more detailed the better, obviously.

I mean, what sort of person could perform such a delicate massage, without some sort of help?

'Just grab it,' he says, so I do. It's as big as I suspected and curving right up to his stomach, so it's not a hard task to accomplish. Although I do run into some trouble almost immediately – my hands are slippery with massage oil without me really intending them to be, and he ... well. He's all messy and leaking, so it's hard to get a good grip. My hand slides and slithers along the length of his shaft, and he makes the most impressive sound.

Like the one I made, not so long ago. Like someone letting go and all that sort of thing.

'Yes,' he says. 'Yes, yes – good girl, oh good girl.'

Which is very nice of him. I don't think I'm doing this very well – my husband was never really one for it, you understand – but he makes sure I know he appreciates it. He even thrusts back and forth into the unsteady but tight circle of my fist, to facilitate matters.

And when that isn't enough, he graciously offers advice.

'Both hands,' he blurts out. 'Use both hands.'

So I do. I get one hand right at the root, and one close and sometimes sliding over the very red tip, and I massage and rub and squeeze. And I suppose I must be doing something right, because his head goes right back and he groans as loud as anything. He *whines* too, which I've never heard before – a very Swedish sounding whine, if there is such a thing, with lots of gasping in between.

'Harder,' he gasps. 'Rub it harder – ah, yes!'

I'm really putting my back into it now. He shows me with his own hands how to twist one this way, while I twist one the other – which sounds really painful, but it makes him say lots of the word *yes*, and the slit at the tip of his prick lets out a little drop of liquid. So I guess he must enjoy it.

Plus it's a real massage, then, isn't it? All this deep twisting and turning, getting all of him in my two small hands. It must be how the real professionals do it, I suppose.

I wonder if the real professionals shake all over, when they do it. And I wonder if their clients shout out, desperately: 'Oh – I'm coming, I'm coming!'

Or maybe that's just him and me.

And he does, you know. He does it all over my thighs, because I've shuffled up very close to him and I'm kneeling like this – so it's very easy for his spend to get all over me. There's a lot of it too, and when he sees what a frightful mess he's made, he seems very embarrassed.

But I tell him not to worry. He can easily clean me up – why, there must be a hundred ways he could go about it! Like lying down on top of me so it all mingles into our skin, sticky and slick at first, but soon rubbed down to nothing.

All over body to body massage, he calls this. I try to tell him that our half-hour is up, but he won't have any of it. 'No,' he says. 'We have to do this.'

So I lie there, while he rubs that rough tunic over my still stiff nipples, and his great bare thighs between my spread legs. He squirms slickly where we're naked, and coarsely where we're not, and sometimes, oh, his body catches mine, just right.

I can feel that thigh, right up against my clit. It's a *very* good massage, this way. So good that we go on for quite a while and I think I might, you know, go over – I'm certainly making quite a bit of noise, which he seems to appreciate.

But then I notice that he appears to be erect again, against my belly. At which point he tells me that he's going to change the massage, slightly. To make it more comfortable for both of us.

I tell him that it's quite comfortable enough for me, but he says no, no, and he looks so pleasant and handsome above me – those pale eyes, suddenly flashing – and he's such a professional, that why should I say no?

And of course, he's right. His prick fits very snugly along the seam of my sex, rubbing through all the slickness I'm sure I should be embarrassed about. I even turn my head to one side, but he says *oh no, no. Don't look away – so pretty*.

He's a good sort. He rubs that big thick head of his cock right over my clit, over and over. Fast, and then slow, and then fast again, and all the while he describes to me how smooth everything is, and wet, and good. He tells me that I'm very good to him, and I think it's those words that make me tingle all over in that breathless, twisting sort of way.

I call out the name which is probably not his, and my clit swells against the press of his cock, and he says *Margot* but pronounces it *Mar-got*, which seems very odd because I thought Margot was a Swedish name.

Though I hardly care if he's got it right or not, because his face is all twisted up and he's panting very hard, again, and I think this all-over-body massage thing is very good indeed, because it wasn't long since he relieved a bit of stress the last time, and he's already going for another.

My husband couldn't go for another after a week, never mind 20 minutes. But then I always said about Sven – he's very skilled. And he must know that sperm is good for the skin, because he's doing it all over me again, right between my legs, all over my clit and my pussy.

I feel it long after he's collapsed on top of me, trickling between the cheeks of my bottom. Or maybe that's just me, because I don't think I've ever had two of those tingles in such a short space of time either.

It's really a testament to his thoroughness. I mean, if there were a performance review to fill out, I know exactly what I'd say. Exemplary employee, really – top marks. Very thorough and professional, always on time and never over stepping his mark.

Not to mention absolutely excellent at making me come.

Would You Like Fries with That?
by Sommer Marsden

FEEL FREE TO LAUGH if you must. I have a friend Charlene who will go on and on when drunk enough about how she loves a man in uniform. Charlene, being a friendly, fun-loving slut, means a Navy uniform, fatigues, police officer, fireman, EMT and the like. I will drink shoulder to shoulder with her, nod and agree. But what I mean by a man in uniform is entirely different.

It isn't much of an issue but for certain days when lunch break takes me out into the bustle and crunch of the city. *Then* it's an issue. I both look forward to and dread these days. I anticipate them wetly and warmly because I know I'm going to get off. I dread them because I know I'll probably end up gaining about a pound from the food.

Today it's McWilliams's. I slip into the warm, neon-lit clatter of the fast-food joint and suck in a breath full of grease and salt and fat. Heaven.

The lines are long. It's lunch time, after all. There are five raggedy lines and a crush of people. The staff look frazzled and overworked but one stands out. He's tall and lanky and barely legal. Definitely graduated because it's a school day and he's here, but not by much. This is probably his college money job and that makes me smile.

His shoulders are broad but still thin from youth, his face is peppered with light stubble and a shock of unruly dark hair pops out from under his regulation cap. I check him head to toe. McWilliams's striped uniform shirt – a white shirt with a navy blue pinstripe. Yellow tie with a tie tack shaped like a burger. A navy cap with the big McWilliams's logo. Dark navy pants, yellow belt and a smile.

I love a man in uniform.

I can't help but fidget with the hem of my dress as I wait in line. Each satisfied customer that passes, I get closer to my server. I can just imagine the starchy feel of his nifty shirt under my fingers as I get him naked. The tinkling jingle of his bright yellow belt complete with logo as I undo it. I shiver, rubbing my thighs together, listening to the subtly sultry whisper of my cable knit tights.

My boots clack over the bright red, not so clean restaurant floor and it's my turn.

'Welcome to McWilliams's,' he says. 'My name is Todd. May I take your order?'

Todd. His name is Todd and he is fabulous. White teeth and red lips. Blue eyes and smooth skin. He must not work the fryer. There isn't a single blemish on his beautiful face. 'Yes, I would like ...' Well hell. What would I like? I have no idea. 'An ... um, chicken sandwich, no condiments. A diet cola and ...' His lips are distracting me and I swallow hard. I can feel the annoyance radiating off the person behind me.

'Ma'am,' he says, exhausted already despite his young age. 'Would you like fries with that?'

'Um ... are they good?'

'For crying out loud!' The woman behind me barks and I turn to her, narrow my eyes.

'Oh, I'm sorry,' I say. 'I was under the impression that it was *my turn*.'

She is frazzled, obese and has three kids in tow. I turn around quickly because I get the feeling she might want to do me bodily harm.

Todd leans in and my pussy twitches at that. Already under my pretty crème-coloured tights, my satin panties are wet in the crotch. My nerves are all jaunty and my skin is buzzing with anxiety and excitement. 'Miss, you really have to order. People tend to get a bit aggressive during the lunch rush,' he says.

'Oh, of course. I would. I would like fries with that.'

Todd nods and smiles. The smile goes straight to my cunt and then swiftly burns a trail from pelvis to nipples. I smile back. When I pay Todd, I slip him the note I brought with me. It's simple, really.

MEET ME IN THE PLAY COURT AT FIVE. I WANT YOU. WEAR YOUR UNIFORM. XOXO J

No phone number. Not even my whole name – Jamie – just orders to meet me if he wants to fuck. It's as simple as burgers, fries and shakes. I walk to the condiment counter and watch him open it. His eyes look up, he searches, finds me. Nod. He smiles again and it is all I can do to eat my chicken sandwich and hurry back to work. I lock myself in the small blue powder room, plant my boot on the toilet lid and push my hand into my panties.

It's Todd the counter boy in his stiff ugly uniform that I see when I rub slippery circles over my clit with my fingertips. I am kissing him, the bill of his McWilliams's hat brushing my forehead as I slide my other hand into my panties and push my fingers into my sopping cunt. I'm grabbing his tie while he fucks me as I get myself off two times, my pussy bunching eagerly around my juicy fingers as I thrust deep into my own body and I come.

I wash my hands, fix my face, and smooth my hair. The rest of the day is all business. My phone rings at three, it's Charlene. 'Meet me for a drink!' she commands. Her voice high and eager and bossy. She makes me laugh.

'I can later. I have to be somewhere at five, but I'm free after that.'

'Ooooh, fancy busy woman. That's fine! Where do you have to be?'

'I have a meeting,' I say and say my goodbyes. Maybe

I'll tell her, maybe I won't. I kind of like having this little secret. This odd little thing that drives me sexually. That makes me fantasize and dream and wonder about what a man has under his ugly fast-food uniform. So far I have been with men from the fish and chips fast-food place, the taco place, the Greek place. Sometimes I like to think of it as an around the world with counter boys. No need to travel. I have a trophy from every stop.

'You look pleased,' Pat says from the doorway.

I start and then laugh. 'Oh, I am. Just having a good, good day,' I say and beam at him.

Pat has hit on me. I don't want him. Not now, anyway. He wears a grey tie and a black suit and wingtips every day. He also frowns a bit, worries and is rushed. I like my men a bit more young. And a bit more colourful in attire. And I like them to offer me a free refill or a baked pie when I order.

I snort, Pat frowns and I give him a finger wave. 'Sorry, back to work.' I shift in my office chair and feel the quiet moist thrill of a woman who has just gotten off and is anticipating doing it again. 'Come on five o'clock,' I breathe and try not to think about what his mouth will taste like.

It tastes like cherry soda and salty fries; his lips are sweet. He pushes me up against the deserted and defaced sliding board and slips his hands into my long brown hair. Such a gentleman, grabbing hunks of hair instead of handfuls of ass. 'Here or in my van?' he asks.

I rear back, pleasantly more excited than I already was. 'You have a van?'

He nods, looking so pleased with himself I almost laugh out loud.

'Here?' I squeak.

'Yes, I do, J – what does J stand for?'

'Oh right, *I* do *not* have a nametag on, do I?' I ask, flicking his shiny gold badge with my finger. 'My name is

Jamie. Nice to meet you,' I say.

He shakes the hand I offer but uses it to pull me in for another kiss. I run my hand up the gorgeously tented blue slacks he has on. I rub the head of his cock through too much fabric with my thumb and he stops kissing me for an instant, his lips still on mine, he just can't manage feeling all that and kissing at the same time. I smile against his soft mouth. 'I like that,' Todd says.

'My name or when I rub your cock like that?' I ask, doing it again.

'Yes,' Todd says and I laugh. He tugs me and my coat gapes open in the sudden wind like I might float away from him. A fairytale princess lifted from earth by gusts of silvery magical air. I squeal playfully and he tugs me harder. Then together we run and slip through the late winter slush to a horribly rusted green van with a small rear window shaped like a spade.

'Smooth,' I tease and he has the good humour to blush and laugh it off.

He opens the rear door and pulls me into the small square cocoon of not quite warmth. It's still chilly as hell but we're out of the wind. His hands are back in my hair, his lips are back on my lips, my fingers are plucking again at the gorgeous hard-on he's sporting.

I pull at his buckle and stop kissing him so I can hear the merry tinkle of the cheap gold fittings on his belt. His dick is long and smooth and so, so warm in my hand. When I squeeze him, he sighs in my ear like a long-time lover. 'Nice?'

'Nice,' Todd says. I can still taste salt on my lips from his kisses, so I dip my head to take the head of his cock into my mouth. His skin's salty taste rivals the fried treat he's eaten today. I suck and he bucks against my mouth gently. Still a gentleman. Still so sweet and nice. A nice young man in a nice shiny uniform with a nice big cock. This time *I* sigh and he pulls me up to kiss me, wrestling with the mess of my tights and my panties. My dress is shoved up, my underthings shoved down and Todd says, 'I wasn't expecting this today.'

'Does it happen other days?' I ask, but I lie back when he pushes me gently. I land in a bundle of blankets and jackets and some more uniforms if I'm not mistaken. My cunt clutches up at that. I wonder if I can beg, borrow or steal a whole shirt and not just some small token when all is said and done. But the thought flies right out of my head when he pushes his lips to my pussy.

'No. Not most days,' he chuckles and then seems to make it his life's mission to lick my clit until I beg. I fist my hands in a blanket and arch my hips up to meet him. He pushes me down with his big hands, he latches to my clitoris and sucks until bright yellow spots fire off behind my closed eyelids.

'You taste like sweet tea,' he laughs. 'Anyone ever told you that?'

I shake my head. No one's ever told me what I taste like period. 'Is that good?'

'Good? Jamie, girl, I could stay here all day.' I come in a long liquid shudder and he just keeps eating me, lapping at me with a tongue that possesses such a talent it has chased all the chill from the hollow, cavernous van.

'Oh, I don't know about all day.'

'All day,' he assures me, drinking me slowly now. Letting my body readjust and calm down and flicker its last bits of release through my pelvis. When my breathing stabilises, he pushes his blunt fingers into my cunt. One, two ... three. I gasp under him as if no one has ever, ever put their fingers in my pussy before. It's almost laughable but it is a new sensation. The intensity that he brings to what he is doing is staggering. And nice, if you really must know.

'I ...'

Todd looks up, tongue still gliding over my pussy lips, my clit, fingers still buried deep inside of me. My mind goes blank. I shrug. I have no idea what I was going to say. He's wiped all logical thought from my head. 'Will you come for me again, Jamie? You really have the sweetest juices,' he says and he grins. His grin is a mix of mischievous boy and the devil. I come for him. I come hard watching him eat me with his long eyelashes brushing his pale cheeks. His face is stunning – a work of art. When he shucks his pants and boxers, I realise that his cock is too.

'Wait,' I say, because he's coming at me and I know, I can tell by his face, that all he wants to do in the world is bury himself in me and fuck. And I want that too, but first ...' Come up here, please.' I whisper.

Out in the parking lot, people are laughing and yelling and dusk is falling because out of his tiny porthole window is the purple air of evening.

He comes up to me, putting his thighs on either side of my arms like I ask. He's basically pinning me that way on my back, arms soldier straight at my sides. His cock slips between my breasts and Todd pushes them firmly together, forming tight cleavage to fuck. Every time he slides high between my tits I lick my tongue out and slide it along the weeping slit at the head of his cock.

He's lost somewhere, I can tell. His face almost shadowed, mesmerized as he watches his own cock slide up between the seam of my breasts and then takes in the sight of my red tongue darting out to meet him. His eyes are blue and wide when he looks at me and says bluntly, 'I'm going to come like a bottle rocket if we keep this up. It's too much.'

I laugh at his honesty. 'OK.'

I tug the shiny pearlescent snaps of his shirt and stroke them like good luck charms. My fingers tickle along the logo stitched on his pocket and I say, 'Ask me something fast foodie.'

Todd pauses but doesn't seem shocked or turned off. You'd be surprised at how often they get flustered and pissed. Instead, he spreads my legs wide and nudges my dripping slit with his cock. 'Um ... let's see, would you like fries with that, Miss?' He thrusts in before I can respond and all of my words fly off when he fills me. His cock has stretched me wide and my pussy is thumping with my pulse. I don't see myself making it long before I come again.

Where has Todd been all my life?

'I would. I would like fries with that.'

He's playing along and I adore him for it. He turns his cap around so that the back logo shows and I tug his tie though only his top button is done. He comes down with a crushing kiss and then nips my ear with his even white teeth. 'Do you need ketchup packets with your fries?' Todd flings my legs high on his shoulder, angles me, fucks me deeper so that I have to struggle to pull a single shuddering breath.

'Oh God, I do. I do need ketchup packets with my fries.'

Todd nods, his face set with concentration as he watches his dick slip into me and then tug free. Slip ... tug ... slip ... tug. 'Do you want relish?'

'I ... I hate relish,' I gasp. My cunt is growing tighter with each thrust. His fingers are so harsh on my skin I want to beg and scream and tell him to hold me tighter.

Instinctively he does. He grips my ankle in one hand, turns his head and nips my ankle with his teeth. 'Would you like a pie for dessert?'

The pain sings up my calf and I shake all over as the orgasm rips through me. He's thrusting hard and fast and his muscles are trembling like it's everything he has not to just come right that instant. 'I would. I would love a pie. I love pie. I loooooooove piiiiiie!' I sing as every flicker and spasm dances through my pussy and I am grabbing his tie and possibly choking him to death.

Todd does not die. Todd pulls free, grabs my ass with both hands and turns me. The secretive sound of fabric being manoeuvred fills the van and then his golden tie drapes around my neck and I am ready to come all over again. 'My name is Todd and I'll be training you, trainee. First order is you must always be in uniform.'

He's rubbing the head of his cock to my pussy from behind and I'm holding my breath. When his hand snakes around and grabs the tail of the tie and slides it around so he can hold it behind my head like a rein, I moan.

Todd pushes into me slowly and then he tugs the tie like a leash. I feel my body grow tight and hot. I hang my head and inhale the smells of him. Young man, aftershave, fryer grease. He's fucking me and tugging that tie until his movements become fast and frenzied. 'You will always be in uniform or there will be a reprimand,' he says.

He tries to sound authoritative. But he sounds like a young man about to shoot his load, but I am on the verge of coming again so I give him a hearty, breathy, 'Yes, sir. I understand, sir.' My fingers are pinching my slippery clit desperately.

'Good,' he says and gives my ass one firm smack. The smack does it for us both. No one is any more good. Todd comes with a roar. I sigh, my fingertips rubbing over my clit until I bear my weight on my forehead alone and come with him. Mine is much more quiet and exhausted.

We sit there in the dark van, breathing hard. Then Todd leans in and kisses me. It is a surprisingly tender, sweet kiss for a hook-up. 'I have something for you,' he says.

I hold my breath, hoping against hope and yes, he hands me a striped McWilliams's shirt. My very own. Not a badge or a hat or a tie or a key-ring. A *shirt*. That I can wear any time I want to remember this. 'Thank you,' I breathe. I kiss him again. I rather like kissing him.

'I don't expect to see you back, but you know where to find me if you want ...' he seems to consider his words. 'A refill,' he says, finally and grins.

I have never wanted a refill before. But I just might want one this time. Todd is not your average counter boy. I kiss him one more time, push my starched prize in my tote and run off into the cold darkness, my body still thumping and quivering like a cooling engine.

'Seriously, you are all glowy. What have you been doing, girl?' Charlene demands, downing her fizzy pink drink.

'Just taking care of myself,' I say quite sincerely. I sip my Merlot and relish the fruity dark flavour on my tongue. I almost imagine I can taste salty fries with it.

A group walks in and Charlene singles out a guy in sailor whites. His crisp white shirt is jaunty with colourful decorations and medals. 'Colonel? Sergeant? Corporal?' she asks me, practically salivating.

I shrug. 'I haven't a clue. They don't make any sense to me.' Now talk to me about burger joint versus taco hut and we're talking my language.

'Whatever,' she says, staring. 'I do love a man in uniform.'

I brush my fingers over the stiff cheap shirt in my purse and smile. 'Me too,' I tell her.

The Arresting Officer
by Justine Elyot

I WISH I HADN'T done it now.

This tree is way, way higher than it looked from the ground, and I think I might be sick – all over the slick blond head of the slick blond cop who is haranguing me from its ancient roots. High principles are one thing – heights are quite another. I should never have mixed them.

But I keep up the fierce pretence, blowing my whistle and giving the rallying cry. 'Save our Spinney!' The raggle-taggle leftovers of my group of friends cheer half-heartedly. Less than a mile away, through the tangled veins of the wood, the bulldozers are visible.

I try to look forward, at them, instead of looking down. My grip on the branch is so tight I think my fingers might cramp and end up joined irrevocably to the wood – which is kind of a nice image. Me and the tree, as one, partners in nature. No, hang on, Imogen. You aren't *that* mad about the environment. If you're honest with yourself, you only did this after a jar too many at the campaign meeting-slash-piss-up last night. Bloody Wormlugs and Gaia, egging me on like that, then claiming they couldn't climb the tree with me because they had to go and sign on. Ah well, fuck 'em. Here I am and here I stay. Not least because I have no idea how to get down. For all my love of trees, I have never technically climbed one before.

Through the rustling leaves and swooping breezes, a male voice almost reaches my ears. I can hear parts of what he says, but there are many gaps.

'... down ... dangerous ... trespass ... arrest you.'

Ugh, it all sounds very unpleasant. If he wants me, he'll have to come and get me. I scrunch one eye up to a slit and risk a downward glance. I was right. He is hot, in an oddly familiar kind of way. Why does the babylon man have to be hot? Why does life have to be complex? Can't we all just live among the trees and sing around campfires and love each other and all that?

'I can't heeeeear yooooou,' I call down in a singsong voice before breaking into a verse of *We Shall Not Be Moved*. What else could I sing? *Blowing in the Wind* seems appropriate somehow. The branches are beginning to lurch and sway alarmingly and my foothold is slipping. Shit. I can't hold on much longer.

'You're going to fall!' bellows PC Broadchest.

'No shit, Sherlock!' I yelp, losing my footing and grabbing frantically at the thickest part of the branch while my legs swing in search of another billet. From the corner of my eye I can see the remnants of the Spinney Action Group posing for the local press photographer, oblivious to my predicament. The only person who seems to care that I am facing a future of quadriplegia is the copper, who is darting around the trunk trying to find a way to help me.

'Imogen!' he shouts. He knows my name. And I know his voice. Oh my God, oh, no way, no way, no ... My shriek of terror rends the air as the branch begins to creak, then to peel slowly and sickeningly away from the tree trunk. The identity of the policeman is forgotten, chased from my brain by the classic life-flashing-before-me sequence. There is crashing, slipping, plunging, scratching of twigs and then arms, strong, male arms breaking my fall, slowing me down to a perfect landing until I am lying on the ground in the tight embrace of a burly uniformed man, my mouth gasping and shrieking into his stab vest.

'I'm alive,' I gibber, raising my head to stare at ... oh

God, this is so incredibly random ... Jason Sargent, my Year 11 boyfriend.

'Yes. But you might not be, by the time I've finished with you,' he says grimly, hauling me to my reluctant feet and encircling my elbow in a strong grip. 'Come on.'

'It's you,' I say, rather unnecessarily. 'And you're a ...' I swallow down the insulting epithet on the tip of my tongue and replace it with, 'police officer'.

'Yep,' he says, marching me off through the woodland paths, leaving the others to do Press Liaison.

'Weird. What happened to you? You were the one who persuaded me to join Greenpeace. And now you're with ... the opposition.'

'I'm not "with the opposition" at all.' I remember that long-suffering, frustrated tone. He used to use it all the time when we were arguing about Science homework. He was usually right, but I just couldn't concede. 'I still have my own beliefs and principles. I just prefer to express them within the law. Unlike you. You think you're above the law, don't you? You always did.'

'No!' I lie. 'I can't believe you want that tree chopped down! You ... don't you remember? That tree ...'

'Yes,' he sighs. 'I remember.'

Our first kiss, playing hookey from the cross-country run, holding hands and laughing all the way to the oaks. He wasn't averse to breaking a rule or two back then.

'If it helps, Imogen, I don't want them to bulldoze the Spinney either. I've written letters of protest to the planning committee and the local paper. But I know that climbing a tree and shouting a slogan isn't going to change anything.'

'It can do!'

'No it can't.'

We are at his car now, on the edge of the woodland in a lay-by close to the bulldozers.

'Where's your partner?' I ask him, noting that it is empty. 'I thought you guys only worked in pairs?'

'I'd just dropped him off when I took this call,' he said. 'Officially, I'm Off Duty. But when the radio came through, I had this funny feeling ...'

He turns and gives me the high-beam head-to-toe once-over. It makes me want to shiver. He looks stern, and yet wistful, and yet exasperated, and yet a little bit like he might still be interested in me. All in all, it's a dynamite combination of expressions, and the full cop regalia is quite the opposite of a turn-off as well. Fancy having to wear a stab vest. How *manly*. And he has little epaulettes on his shoulder – I guess he is some kind of ranking babylonian.

'Jason Sargent, all grown up,' I say slowly, relishing the words almost as much as I relish the sight of him in that uniform, black and white and hot all over. Something important occurs to me. 'Oh my God, are you a Sergeant? Sergeant Sargent?'

He rolls his eyes. 'Don't start. I've heard it all before. Promoted last week, so every single deathless witticism is fresh in my memory.'

Something else important occurs to me. 'So, um, am I under arrest?'

'You do not have to say anything,' he says, and I gasp with horror. 'But I'll be bloody flabbergasted, knowing you, if you don't.' My breath catches up with me. He is *joking*. Catch yourself on, Imojims. Oh. Imojims. That's what *he* used to call me. Nobody else has called me that in the intervening eight years since I snogged another boy at the post-GCSE disco. 'No, I don't think I'm going to charge you,' he says, leaning back against the car and frowning at me. 'Though I am tempted. What on earth were you thinking, Imogen? What are you *ever* thinking?'

At the moment I'm thinking ... do you have handcuffs? So that's what I say.

He shakes his head, staring at me, almost through me, with limpid lustrous eyes of blue.

'Of course I have handcuffs. Do you have a brain?'

Yeah, but it's located a bit further south than usual just now. I don't say that one out loud.

'I think I must have lost it, to dump you for Robbie Manning.'

He shuts his eyes for a long, long moment. Lovely spidery eyelashes.

'All right, Imogen,' he says robustly, opening his eyes again, back to Action Man in full effect. 'I'm arresting you for wanton flirtation with an officer of the law. You do not have to say anything, but it may harm your defence if you do not mention, when questioned, something which you later rely on in court. Or in bed. Anything you do say may be given in evidence. Evidence that you want me to abuse my position of authority and perform acts of ... what's the word ...?'

'Lewd behaviour?'

'Yeah, exactly. Lewd behaviour. Acts of lewd behaviour. Upon your person. Is that a fair summary?'

'It's a fair cop, guv.' I hold out my wrists, biting my lip, having to jut out a hip to prevent things getting too wet and squirmy between my legs. I nearly moan with arousal when he whips out the cuffs and clicks them smartly on before bundling me into the passenger seat of the car and getting in himself.

'I can't take this home,' he says, seemingly thinking aloud. 'I have to drop it off at the station. And get changed there. And then walk home ... or take you home ... maybe get a taxi ...'

'Oh, but your uniform,' I protest over the gunning of the engine. 'I want you to take me down to the cells.'

'Imogen! I can't do that!'

'I bet you could. I bet you could slip me past the duty officer and get me into an empty cell and ... y'know ...'

'The cells aren't nice, Imogen.'

'What about an interview room? You could interrogate me ... and then when I didn't give up the information ... you could put pressure on me ... over the table ... with your big truncheon ... ohhhh yes ...'

'Jesus, Imogen. You weren't like this when you were 16.'

'No. But the sight of you in your enforcer gear ... mmmm. And these handcuffs feel so heavy. Oh my, I am trapped in your power, Sergeant!'

Twenty minutes later, I sit, still cuffed, slumped in a plastic chair in an interview suite.

'You had better be bloody quiet,' Jason warns me, locking the door behind us. 'These rooms are usually pretty vacant at this time of day, but I've asked Nicki at the front desk to come and give us a knock if there's a risk of disturbance. She's a good sort. She'll cover for me.'

'I hope so.' I beam up at him as he takes a seat opposite me, then remember to get back into role. Sulky uncooperative suspect faced with powerful, sexy, authoritative man wearing a big utility belt. The stuff of illicit fantasies. 'And before you ask, no comment.'

He recovers well from a flicker of bemusement and leans across the scuffed table, banging it with his fist.

'I'll break you, Imogen Lovell, if it takes me all day and all night. Where are the secret plans?'

'NO comment!' I flick a V at him, which is not easy when your wrists are weighed down by several pounds of heavy metal.

'Right, that does it. Time for the strip search. Get on your feet.'

'Make me,' I grouse. He does. He comes around behind me and yanks me out of the chair, kicking it aside before patting his hands down the length of my body, airport security style, but with a substantially increased accompanying frisson. Finding nothing, he pulls my sweater up over my bra and peers inside the cups for contraband.

'Only my nipples there, Sergeant,' I taunt. 'Is that not what you're looking for?'

'I thought they were bullets,' he says gruffly. 'My mistake. Might as well get this off anyway.' He unclips the bra, pulls the sweater over my head and tries to wrestle them over the handcuffs, but to no avail – so they have to remain there, bunched and hanging off my wrists while my upper body is bared and vulnerable to the explorations of his big, brawny hands. He presses them into my breasts, squeezing and fiddling, tickling my nipples until I squirm and try to break free. But he is far, far too strong for that.

'Nothing to hide there,' he decides. 'But I bet I'll find something I'm looking for down here.' He has my jeans unbuttoned in an instant, and he wrenches them down to my ankles before hooking his thumbs into the waistband of my knickers. 'Well, Miss Lovell? Anything to confess before I have to force the issue?'

I shift from foot to foot, acutely aware of my ankles and wrists restrained by denim and metal respectively, embarrassed by the stain of arousal he will doubtless see and approve of when he denudes my privates of their scanty covering.

'I am strangely attracted to you, officer,' I admit. He laughs and pulls down my knickers. The invasive section of the body search commences with three of his fingers dipped in my copious juices.

'So you are,' he murmurs victoriously. 'You're soaking wet down here. Well, I think I know just how to deal with you now.'

I pivot forward, loving the feel of his exploratory fingers, just on the right side of harsh as they twiddle my clit and slide backwards towards the hidden depths.

'Anything to declare up here?' he asks lightly, spearing my cunt with two thick fingers. 'Oh, no, there is nothing hidden here. And you can't hide the fact that you want me to fuck you either. I've never known a hornier dissident.'

I giggle. 'No, I bet you haven't. Oh, officer, please don't!' I exclaim, remembering that I probably shouldn't be quite so happy with the situation.

'So if the secret plans aren't up here,' he says, finger-thrusting energetically while he pushes me down over the desk with a clank of cuffs. 'Where are they?'

'I don't know!' I cry feverishly. The metallic fetters press into my breasts, cold and hard, reminding me of my helpless condition.

'Tell me!' One big flat hand crashes down on my unprepared bottom. I yelp so loudly that Jason retrieves a handkerchief from his pocket and stuffs it into my mouth. 'Quiet!' he scolds before laying on more hard smacks. How unfair! How am I supposed to confess now? Even if I want to?

After a dozen or so, he frees my speech, explaining, 'You can confess now. I just couldn't resist watching your arse change colour first.'

'You swine! What do I get if I don't confess?'

'More of the same, but this time I'll use my belt.'

'Eep. What do I get ... if I *do* confess?'

'What every good girl gets.' Jason crouches and gives my clit the quickest, merest flicker of tongue before straightening up and pressing down in the small of my back. 'You get to come. How's that? Does that work for you? Are you a carrot or a stick girl?'

Hmm, a bit of both, I think.

'I'm not sure,' I tell him. 'Try me with a bit more of the stick. I might not be ready for the carrot yet.'

'Right.' I hear one of my favourite sounds in the world – the unbuckling of a belt – and reflect that Jason Sargent *certainly* wasn't like this when he was 16. If he had been, Robbie Manning could have gone and taken a flying leap, that's for sure. 'Last chance to sing like a canary, Imogen,' he warns me. 'Before I make you howl like a wolf.'

My teeth gritted into the handkerchief, which he has replaced in my mouth, I await the first stroke. Oh, he does it perfectly – just in the right spot, no inconvenient wrapping around the hip, no irritating too-light tickle – just one sweet, smarting stroke to the dead centre of my proffered bottom. Six snaps light me up – as if I wasn't incandescent enough already – before he lays the leather down in front of my nose, takes out my makeshift gag and speaks into my ear.

'I'm going to fuck you. Any objections?'

'None,' I breathe. 'You're the law.'

'Yes, I am.'

Only the trousers and pants mar his impeccably-uniformed exterior, dropped to the knees to facilitate his planned penetration of me. The jeans and knickers binding my ankles mean that I can't spread my thighs too wide, but he seems to enjoy my predicament, pushing his hard cock between my shaking legs, forging a passage through the flesh and into the willing, waiting wet centre of me.

'So tight,' he pronounces. 'And completely under me, completely unable to get away from me. Just as you should be.' He thrusts hard, almost painfully, and with a sharp pang that is not only physical, I realise that he is thinking of the post-GCSE disco. It is payback time for that teenage indiscretion, I realise, but I owe it to him, and I'm not sure payback was ever meant to be quite so pleasurable anyway.

'You're going to behave yourself from now on, aren't you?' he grunts, keeping the motions slow and steady enough that I can still breathe, just about.

'Yes, officer,' I assure him.

'No more climbing up trees, Imogen. And no more flirting with random policemen.'

Oh! He is not playing any more. He is asking a serious question.

'Can't promise ... that last one ...' I gasp.

'Bad girl!' he chides. 'Non-random policemen are, of course, fine. Provided that they are police sergeants with big cocks who know how to make you come over and over again. Do you know any of those?'

'Have a feeling ... I might do ...'

His cock feels so huge and swollen between my clamped thighs, every back and forth movement dragging the sensitive inner skin. The angle means that his tight, hard balls bounce against my clit with every stroke, and the sensation builds, very slowly at first, then higher and higher and higher and higher until I bang my cuffs on the table and begin to wriggle furiously, pushing myself back on his impaling rod and biting down on the chain link between the cuffs to muffle the long, low howl of climax I want to release.

'Take it!' he snarls, plunging in to the hilt and pumping his punishing seed into me, delirious with the power and the pleasure.

'Now then,' he says, a few minutes later, slumped over me on the desk. 'About those secret plans ...'

I chuckle into the graffiti-pocked wood.

'I'll never surrender,' I murmur weakly.

'Looks like I'll have to apply a bit more pressure then. At my place. Tied to my bed, naked, for the rest of the day. Are you ready for that?'

'Oh, officer, spare me!' But I don't mean it. And he knows it.

I am, as promised, tied to his bed naked, spreadeagled on my back with a vibrator humming inside me, writhing and twisting in my fourth orgasm of the day, when his phone rings.

'Oh really?' he says, letting the soft suedey ribbons of a flogger drift over my breasts and belly as he speaks. 'That's excellent news. Fantastic. Thanks, Councillor. Thanks for letting me know.'

Through the mists of mind-blowing climax, I hear him put the phone down and feel him prod at my belly with the flogger.

'Are you back with us yet?' he asks lightly. 'I've got some good news for you.'

'Nnnrrrrgh?' I query, realising that he has well and truly had his revenge on me for the Robbie Manning incident. I doubt I will ever walk again.

'Yes. Nnnrrrrgh,' he says, smiling. 'Or rather, the Spinney is saved. Councillor Lewis and I looked into the possibility of Tree Preservation Orders. Looks like they've been granted, right at the last minute. The bulldozers are going to have to turn tail and go home.'

'Wow, thass mazin,' I say, my tongue feeling all huge and furry in my mouth. Jason tilts a glass of water to my lips. 'Really cool. I didn't know you were so influential.'

'I'm not. I just know the law.'

'Because you are the law.'

'You said it. Now can I take this uniform off?'

'For now. Until next time.'

'You'd better pray I never apply to become a detective.'

'Oh, I will. Every day.'

Solitary Confinement
by Lily Harlem

I'VE BEEN BAD, REALLY bad ... jail-time bad. Fraud, embezzlement, perverting the course of justice, you name it I've done it.

When Lucy Trill Employment Agency collapsed two years ago I couldn't risk losing my dream home. Temptation became too damn tempting and I improvised to save that white picket fence, wraparound veranda and kitchen so big and shiny I could see my reflection in the marble work surface.

Sitting now two years later at a chipped Formica table secured to the floor it couldn't have worked out more perfectly, in fact, I don't regret a thing.

I stare at my jailhouse dinner. Grey mush, green mush, orange mush and a stale roll, no butter. Hardly five star. Trinny is wittering on again, talking with her mouth full – she drives me nuts, always on about her innocence. If she was innocent she wouldn't be here, it's simple; we're all guilty, we're all paying the price, we're all getting what we deserve.

I shovel in a few tasteless mouthfuls knowing I'll need my strength later. I knock back the mush with a slug of water and glance at the clock over the door. It's an hour past change of shift so it shouldn't be long now.

I rest my spoon down, pull my chestnut curls into a pony tail and snap a band to secure it to my nape. My heart is fluttering in my chest like a captive butterfly. I'm not sure if I can pull this off. It could go horribly wrong.

I sense Colt's arrival before my eyes even fall in his direction. It's as though his heavy, male presence changes the flow of energy around the place. It circles me, embraces me, it makes the blood pool between my legs and tightens my bare nipples against my scratchy orange top.

I risk a sideways glance and spot him with a junior colleague, a brooding look on his angular face. He stands with his black boots hip width apart, broad shoulders squared and arms crossed over his chest. His navy uniform looks freshly pressed and the gold writing on his short sleeves strains over his biceps. The shiny brown belt he always wears holds handcuffs, a baton and a mobile phone. Being senior warden he also has a huge set of silver keys which I know from watching him endlessly, swing against his groin as he walks, tapping on the single pleat of his navy trousers, swaying and caressing just where I imagine his dick to be.

My mouth waters for the first time since I came to dinner.

I look at Trinny again, think how ugly she is with her lank straw hair, pimples and missing teeth, and then I go for it. I slide my hands beneath my dinner tray, leap up and fling it in her direction with a scream of, 'Shut up, bitch.'

Pandemonium breaks out.

It's as though humans have turned into warring animals. Trinny doesn't even wait for the sloppy food to begin its slide down her face and immediately hurtles her tray back at me. I dodge to the left only to find myself pushed in front of her again by a surge of excited women chanting, 'Fight, fight, fight.'

Trinny is up on the table, squatting like a coiled cobra with her lips pulled back over shiny pink gums. I clench my fists, ready to take her on, ready for anything.

I wish he'd hurry up.

She pounces towards me and I stumble as her weight

lands on my chest. I manage to scrape my nail over her cheek and drag a handful of her hair into a fist. I tug – more than half falls out.

Where the hell is he?

She screeches like a banshee. I grunt and throw a punch into her kidney. She sends a fist back and it rockets into my solar plexus. I screw up my eyes as air surges from my lungs.

Suddenly enormous, solid hands wrap around my waist. I'm pulled sharply back and my spine connects with a wide, concrete chest. A stubbled chin presses into my temple and hot, fast breath shoots down my neck.

I open my eyes, drag in much needed oxygen and make an effort to appear as though I'm struggling against the guard. As soon as my breath is back I hurl a string of colourful abuse at Trinny.

Trinny is really going for it, she's so wild two prison officers have tackled her to the ground and her orange limbs are flailing wildly. But Colt is big, much bigger than his two junior staff so it's not remarkable that he can hold my slight frame without breaking sweat.

'Show's over, ladies,' his deep voice vibrates deliciously from his chest onto my back. 'Sit and eat.' He keeps his arms locked around me, pinning my arms to my sides as he sweeps an authoritative gaze around the room.

The sea of women disperses and the normal hum of conversation resumes. Trinny – still yelling – is hauled to her feet and dragged away.

'Get the hell off me, she started it,' I shout wriggling my hips and shoulders against him in a wild dance.

'Don't give me that crap, I saw the whole thing.'

He rams me harder against his body.

I catch my breath and freeze; his erection is as solid as a rod of steel ramming into the hollow of my back.

'You're off to solitary,' he says grinding harder into me. 'Twenty-four hours.'

A few ladies tip their heads in sympathy for my plight, but I look away, I don't want it. Solitary was exactly what I'd been hoping for, except it won't be solitary, at least not all the time.

He manoeuvres me into the crook of his shoulder and lightning fast captures my wrists in cool handcuffs. I roll my shoulders and snap my hands apart as if furious when in reality a thrill is surging through my body and sparking my nerve-endings like an electric shock.

He shoves me a half pace in front of him and I stumble towards the canteen door. I have to force myself not to run so eager am I for that solitary cell.

We leave the noisy chatter of the canteen and he imprisons my upper arm in his hand and drags me down the deserted corridor. My breaths are heavy, so are his. Our footsteps clatter like bullets in a barrel and I stumble to keep up with his ground-eating paces.

'Good show, Lucy,' he mutters throwing a wary glance over his shoulder. 'Very believably bad.'

'Thanks,' I whisper, delighted by his praise.

'So you gonna take your punishment like a big girl?'

'Yes, yes, I will.'

A ghost of a smile tips his lips and his black eyes sparkle with a combination of both lust and amusement. 'Good,' he husks tipping his head closer to mine. ''Cause you've been very bad today, very bad indeed.'

I practically whimper in anticipation and have to lean onto his body as my knees turn boneless. I've been bad plenty of times, but I've never been "very" bad before!

Another three corridors and through two locked metal gates and we're outside solitary cell number one. He lets go of my arm and reaches for his keys. He doesn't have to worry about me running away, the only place I'm running is in that big, bare room with its grey, block walls, single metal framed bed and small white potty in the corner.

He pushes at the steel door and glances over his

shoulder again. 'In,' he orders using the flat of his hand to keep the heavy door from slamming shut. 'Quick.'

I scurry in. I might combust in a minute I'm so turned on. I yank against the handcuffs, glance around the windowless room and notice a single white candle on the fibrous grey bedcover.

I'm about to ask if he's planning a romantic meal when suddenly his colossal body hits. Together we stumble against the wall. His urgent lips connect with mine and his tongue invades my mouth. Two big hands cup my buttocks and squeeze to the point of pain.

I groan in delight and let his weight pin me against hard bricks, my hands still trapped behind my back. His all-male taste and sharply spiced scent invade my poor deprived senses. He's such a raw dose of testosterone and I know he'll leave me with a full tank of satisfaction – I can't wait for him to start filling me up.

His hands travel to the elastic waist of my orange trousers and he shoves them down to my knees – they fall the rest of the way. I kick them from my feet and quickly step out my flat pumps. He swipes a hand around my waist searching for my knickers, intent no doubt on ripping them from my body.

But there's no need for him to search. I'm not wearing knickers.

He pulls his head back far enough to look into my eyes. 'Oh, you're so bad.' He pulls at his bottom lip with his tooth. 'So, so bad.'

I arch an eyebrow. 'Are you complaining, officer?'

'Hell no.' He grabs for his keys and with a practised twist unlocks the handcuffs and tosses them onto the bed.

My hands delight in their new freedom and travel over his body, my palms soak up the hard heat radiating through his work clothes and my fingers muss through his short turf of dark hair.

I'm interrupted in my exploration as he drags my nasty

orange top over my head. I watch it land on the dirty floor and pause for a second to relish being completely naked and free from the relentlessly itchy material.

He groans at the sight of my exposed breasts and dips his head to suck on my left nipple. His calloused hand cups soft flesh and he feeds it into his mouth like a starving man. The roll of his tongue elongates my peaked nipple and I arch like a bow towards him, fluttering my eyes shut and moaning in ecstasy.

Next thing I know he's swung me against his chest and is striding towards the bed. I open my eyes and look at him. His face has a determined, predatory look to it. I shiver; I haven't seen him this urgent in his passion before. This week's performance must have really rocked his boat.

He tips me onto the bed and I land on all fours facing the pock-marked, grimy wall. I catch in my rapidly expelled breath and go to spin round.

'No,' he growls, shoving a hand between my bare shoulder blades. 'Stay like that. Keep your bad little ass in the air.'

I hear the rattle of handcuffs by my ear. He looms over me and neatly catches my wrists in the loops again. But before he snaps shut the left one he hooks it through a thin metal slat on the side of the frame, effectively harnessing me to the bed.

'Colt, I ...'

'Shut it,' he warns.

'But ...' There's a tremble of both delight and trepidation in my voice.

'This is what you deserve,' he says and I hear him wrestling with his belt and flies. 'So make the most of it, jail bait.'

His mouth lands in the small of my back and he presses urgent kisses and sweeping licks down the crack of my buttocks. The sharp stubble on his chin creates a trail of fire that's deliciously sore.

His tongue travels lower and probes at the tight rose bud of my anus. I jerk in reflex and yank against the handcuffs. Big hands clamp over my hip bones. 'Keep fucking still,' he mutters.

His kisses move down further and he nuzzles into my pussy. A quiver of bliss snakes up my spine and I sigh and hang my head, making sure I keep my pelvis perfectly still. His tongue swirls at my entrance lapping the juices collecting for him. I spread my knees wider, flaunting my sex and inviting him in.

Suddenly his teeth sink into my left butt cheek, hard and fast. Then several more sharp bites spread over both orbs.

I gasp in surprise and squirm. Trying to get away from the pain but somehow wanting more. It's so shockingly good.

Then the teeth have gone and a sharp slap replaces the pinching sensations. It hits like a jellyfish sting and then blooms to a fiery ache. I moan and buckle my elbows. I'm so glad I've been bad.

His palm connects again, on the other butt cheek this time, firm and prompt. I feel the whoosh of air a nanosecond before it connects and delight in that moment of anticipation. Once again the pain is both beautifully erotic and toe-curlingly terrible and I ride its scrumptious journey across my delicate flesh. They're not gentle taps; they hurt and the pain hums straight to my clit.

'You handling your punishment, bad girl,' Colt grunts from somewhere behind me.

'Yes, yes,' I say pressing my backside towards where I imagine him to be standing. 'Please ... more.' I need him inside me so bad I could scream with frustration. I tug my hands and hear the tinny rattle of metal on metal. It's no good, I'm at his mercy.

'Don't you worry, there's much more in store for you,' he says.

Finally I feel the smooth head of his penis against my

pussy, he swirls it around the soft, wet folds coating it in my natural lube. He hovers over my clit then increases the pressure and treats me to a slow, steady rotation right where I need it; the sensation creates a tug in the pit of my stomach and I buck back for more, cursing the containment of the cuffs once again.

'Please,' I say desperately. 'Colt just be a man and fuck me.'

He chuckles, a deep guttural sound that tells me just how much he's enjoying his power over me. I wonder when he'll let me have it. When he'll give me what I deserve.

I don't have to wonder for long, because with a sudden, heaving thrust his dick charges into me, right to the hilt. His forest of coarse pubes rams up against my butt and his tensed thighs connect with the back of mine. I'm stretched wide width ways and pushed to the limit length ways and I cry out in absolute delight. The feeling of being impaled by him is so consuming, so utterly perfect. I could stay like this for ever.

'Fuck, yes,' he hisses, his left hand leaving my hip to duck round my belly and fret my clit. He works it hard and fast, slow and deep, then hard and fast again.

I gasp at his wickedly accurate touch and sink onto him, drumming my feet over the side of the bed and grabbing for the orgasm I know is within reach.

He sets up a pounding pace and I feel like he's filling not just my pussy but right up to my head. Just when I think it can get no better I feel his other hand exploring the crack of my butt again. I close my eyes only to be greeted with a pyrotechnic display of fireworks. Have I been *that* bad?

It seems I have.

His finger closes in on my anus and I feel it pressing in the centre of the tight band of quivering muscle.

I whimper and fist the rough blanket in my trapped hands. I know what's coming, he's done this to me twice before.

He grunts something incoherent, stills his hips and pushes his thick finger in.

I feel the cords on my neck strain as my head flies back. The sensation is scorching on barely used muscles and totally overwhelms the fire created from the spanking. He gains further entry and I force myself to open up for the long, smooth touch of him. It's so wicked, so carnal, so utterly dirty this road to satisfaction we're indulging in.

But suddenly it doesn't feel right. It's longer than a finger, cooler, smoother. I'm confused.

'What ...' I twist to look, instinct causing my body to buck and wrestle with the cuffs.

'Keep still,' he mutters again.

'But what is ...' I force my body to calm. I trust him.

'It's the candle,' he says. 'It's your punishment, Lucy. You have to take your punishment up the ass.'

'Now who's being naughty ...?' I manage before my words break into a long, low sigh as his dick slides into my pussy in time with the slow slip of the candle. His fingers brush over my clit again and the feeling shoots through my vagina to my full ass causing me to clench and shake.

I want so much more.

Colt picks up the pace again. He gives short sharp thrusts and each pound sends the candle deeper into me as his body rams onto mine. It goes higher, filling me more and more. My thighs and belly go tight and a desperate moan escapes my lips. I'm going to come.

My clit strains beneath the pads of his fingers as I'm suspended in a blissful state. My vision blurs, blood screams through my ears and every fibre of my being is tensed like a taut elastic band. I imagine what I look like tied naked on the bed with my spanked red ass high in the air, a big dick ramming into me and a candle shoved up my rectum.

This filthy, erotic image sends me over the edge and with a snap I come crashing down. With violent force the climax rips wildly through my body.

I hear him grunt as his cock goes as hard as it can possibly go. His forearms tighten around me, holding me exactly where he wants me. I feel my pussy contracting around his dick and my back-hole spasming around the candle, seizing it as I ride the orgasm rollercoaster.

He moves one hand to my hip and the other to my shoulder and grips me, driving in deeper and harder and causing me to gasp as he forges even further in. All that unharnessed, raw power blasting into me sends me over the edge again. This time it's my g-spot in charge and I peak into another deeply satisfying orgasm that explodes from within. Shockwaves career over my tattered body and my elbows finally collapse onto the bed.

But he's not quite done and I keep my ass in the air as he takes his own pleasure. Fucking me like there's no tomorrow. His breathing is harsh and hot on my back and then suddenly it stops.

He freezes, everything is still.

I can picture his face contorted in a Neanderthal type grimace as he tips his neck to the ceiling.

And then I feel it, hot semen spurting up to my womb, flooding my body, possessing me.

He begins to move again, tight little jerks of his hips. 'Fuck, that's so good,' he groans. His grip loosens on my shoulder and his hands sweep down my sweat damp skin. 'You are so damn hot, Lucy, I could fuck you like this every day for the rest of my life.'

I nod, too weak to converse properly.

His cock slides out my pussy and he tugs at the base of the candle. As he withdraws it I feel my hole re-tighten. I flop sideways and curl up in the foetal position.

'You OK?' he asks tossing the candle under the bed and doing up his trousers.

'Mmm,' I say letting a contented smile settle on my lips. 'More than OK.'

The bed dips as he reaches across me and undoes the

handcuffs. He lifts my wrists, kisses the redness then rubs my small hands in his enormous ones to encourage the flow of blood.

'I can stay for another ten minutes,' he says. 'Before I'm missed.'

I look up at his face; he has beads of sweat on his brow and top lip and his pupils are wide. 'Lie with me,' I say, stretching out my nakedness, unwilling to reclaim my torturous clothing until I have to.

He grins and stretches on the narrow bed, dragging me on top of him so we can both fit on the meanly thin mattress. I tangle my legs with his and snuggle into his shoulder, pushing two fingers through a button hole on his shirt so I can swirl his chest hair. The air is cool but his body is hot, the perfect combination for my frazzled nerve-endings.

'I painted your front fence on my day off,' he says, tracing a lazy pattern on my tender, still smarting backside.

'You did?'

'Yeah, it was peeling and I want it nice for when you go home.'

'Thanks, that was thoughtful.' I lean up and press a soft kiss to his lips.

'I'm a thoughtful guy,' he murmurs onto my mouth.

'Yeah, I know.' I think of the candle. 'Very thoughtful.' I kiss him again. 'Have you moved your stuff in yet?'

'No, next weekend.'

'Oh,' I say, pulling up so I can look into his eyes.

'Don't panic,' he laughs. 'You've got three whole weeks until you're in the real world again.' He releases my pony tail and runs his fingers through my hair, spreading it over my bare shoulders and down to my breasts. 'Plenty of time for me to get organised and move out my flat, I'll be there.' He holds my head steady over his. 'I promise.'

I sigh and tip my head into the cradle of his palm. 'I know, I'm just so looking forward to us being a real couple without all this subterfuge, and I'm afraid something will go wrong when we're so near the end of my time.'

'Nothing will go wrong, how can it when I love you and you love me?'

My heart swells like a balloon. I adore hearing him say those three words; he rolls them around his tongue like syllables to be savoured and then pours them out into the air like the sweetest honey on the planet.

'We can still play games though, right?' he asks, his heavy brows lifting and his eyes delving into mine.

'Of course, we can be even more imaginative when there's no need for elaborate plans just to snatch a few minutes together, not to mention a big, soft bed and all the time in the world. ' I widen my eyes. 'I might get you to keep your uniform on sometimes though – just to remind me of our first time.'

He laughs and I know the image of us fucking wildly in the linen room is crossing his mind. 'Mmm, but the next time you see a candle it's going to be in a restaurant, over dinner, when we go on our first date.'

'To be fair I didn't exactly see much of the candle.' I tug at my lip with my tooth.

'True.'

'But still, I'm looking forward to our first date.' I smile and snuggle back into his shoulder.

'Yeah, I've booked Gianni's for the evening of the 21st. They do amazing carbonara with mussels and a secret recipe key lime pie that's just to die for.'

My taste buds tighten at the thought. 'That sounds great.'

'It is.' Colt goes quiet but I sense words stalling on his lips.

'What's up?' I ask.

'I'm going to get the box room cleared and painted before you get out too.'

'You are?'

'Yeah, I was thinking a pale lemon might be nice.'

'Why lemon?' I glance up, amused by his sudden determinedness.

'Because.' He runs a hand to my belly and presses very gently. 'It would be the perfect colour for a nursery.'

End of the Line
by Heidi Champa

MOVING TO THE CITY had meant giving up many things, but my car was the first thing to go. There was no place to park it at my new apartment, and paying for a space clear across town seemed pointless. So, I bid it farewell, and sold it to a new and hopefully loving owner. It would be public transportation for me from then on. While I missed the joys of singing along to the radio and putting on my make-up at stoplights, at least I could console myself with the idea that I was helping to save the environment. After all, having an ancient gas-guzzler hardly fit with the new life I was trying to lead.

I stood on the narrow swath of cement, waiting for the Number 91 tram. Every day since I arrived in the city, it was the same routine. The 7.40 a.m. and the 5.17 p.m. The trams were usually on time, not like the buses. That was a lesson I learned the hard way. After being late for work three days in a row, I knew I had to find another way to navigate the winding streets of my new environment. So, I started waiting for the loud, rumbling cars every morning, and I haven't missed a single meeting since.

The trams also provided an added bonus I hadn't counted on. Every Monday, Thursday and Friday, I got to ride home with Stella. She was gorgeous, even in the awful blue-grey transit authority uniform. It seemed a crime to put someone so beautiful into something so ugly, but somehow it didn't seem to matter. Her sewn-on nametag stuck out from under her long dark hair, and from the first day I read her name, Stella was burned on to my brain. I always sat at the front of the car so I could stare at her through the glass partition.

I had only spoken to her once, but that was all it took. It was the first day I stepped on the tram; the very first time I saw her perfect face. I realised I didn't know how the ticket system worked, and I panicked a bit before biting the bullet and asking for help. I tapped on the little windowed compartment and Stella turned and gave me a nod.

'How much for the weekly pass?' I smiled. Her blue eyes were so distracting, I almost forgot why I was standing there. She smiled back, her rose pink lips stretching over her almost too-perfect teeth.

'The machine is right back there, it will give you the ticket. The weekly pass is $7.50.'

She wasn't impatient or angry. She didn't even give me the look of pity that the rest of the city folk had perfected for people like me. Just that smile. I almost stumbled, my high heel slipping on the grooved walkway as the tram lurched forward. I recovered and headed back to the machine to buy my ticket, fumbling with my dollars as I tried to remain cool and calm despite my pounding heart. After that, I was hooked. But, I never talked to her again. There was no legitimate reason for me to engage her, despite my efforts to think of one. So, I had to be content to look at her, and admire her from afar.

Since that first day, I had become an expert with a monthly pass, like most of the people around me. I was a regular. Every day that Stella drove, we would share a smile and I would sit and watch her through the glass. Occasionally, she glanced my way, in her casual, offhand manner. When she did, I felt my body tighten and my insides turn to mush. Being new to the city, I didn't have many friends. Stella managed to make me feel less alone, without ever saying a word. Somehow, knowing she was there made me feel like I had someone to count on, even though we were strangers.

Over time, I started to learn my way around the city and actually ventured out beyond my little neighbourhood. I even managed to convince a few friendly people that I wasn't a total hick. No small feat with the accent I had. Even with my newfound comfort and community, Stella remained my touchstone. During those rides home, I couldn't stop glancing her way, looking at her lovely profile and trying to grow the courage to say something, anything to her. As we screeched our way through the city over the tramlines, I couldn't help but wonder what her lips might taste like or how her hands might feel on my body. Stella started to dominate my fantasies, and it proved to be a great way to pass the time on my lengthy commute back to my empty apartment, and it returned every time I saw Stella at the helm.

The gentle sway of the tram car soothed me and after a long look at Stella, I closed my eyes, and let my mind fill with thoughts of her. In my head, I saw her delicate fingers opening the buttons of her drab uniform, moving her fingers slowly and seductively, making the ugly city-issued garment seem enticing and sexy. The transportation authority had no idea what they had done when they put someone as amazing as Stella in that uniform. Her eyes never left mine as she stripped for me, moving her hips with the grace of a burlesque dancer. The uniform that she wore would never have been mistaken for a sexy outfit. But, it covered Stella, and that fact made it one of the hottest things I'd ever seen.

The grey fabric slowly fell away, revealing that she was wearing nothing underneath; no bra or panties stood in the way of me seeing all of her. I pictured the curves of her breasts, the colour and shape of her nipples, imagining their deep brown shade and puckered texture as I slouched a little further into my seat. I filled in the blanks of her whole body; the swell of her hips and the thick dark hair between her legs. Stella didn't strike me as the type to be shaved or waxed. Her body was always so hidden from me, covered by thick cotton fabric that didn't show me nearly enough of her shape. But that didn't stop my dirty mind from providing every last detail of what I knew had to be a beautiful body.

My tongue moved inside my mouth, desperate for the chance to run over the stiff peaks that teased my brain but in real life stayed hidden under her uniform. The desire to taste her had consumed me since I'd first seen her. I opened my fists, my fingers stiff in my lap as my pussy flooded with heat, my mind's eye thick with visions of my hands on her firm, trembling stomach as I sucked hungrily on her nipples. I could almost taste her, the flavour of her skin enticing on my tongue.

My mind fixed on a gorgeous mental picture of Stella, head thrown back, moaning my name in ecstasy as I teased her nipples and dropped my hand between her legs. My fingers slid through her curls, damp from her excitement, and found her pussy soaking wet and hot. I could almost smell her exhilaration. Her hips came up to meet me, making me go deeper inside her hot pussy, making her moans deeper and louder. Her voice turned breathy and soft in my ear, her tongue sweeping lightly over my skin. Her hand rested over mind, making me speed up, bringing her closer and closer to her peak. I envisioned her pressing my thumb against her clit, strumming it lightly in the same rhythm as my plunging fingers. I could imagine it hard and slick under my touch, feel it swell as Stella got more excited. I would have given anything to see her that way, to have her respond to me that way.

I could feel the heat becoming unbearable between my legs and I bit my lip to keep quiet. My mind was overloaded by my hallucinations, but I didn't want it to end. I knew I was enjoying my fantasy a bit too much, so it was just as well the noise of the tram on the tracks cut through my hot and hazy thoughts and brought me back to reality. My face felt flushed and I cast a quick glance to Stella, her eyes peering out the window into the night in front of us, just like always. I watched her for a few more moments waiting for a smile, but it didn't come.

One Friday night, I waited patiently for the tram so I could finally head home from work. My stomach contracted, as it always did, as the #91 pulled up to the stop. All I could think about was Stella's soft blue eyes I would soon see staring back at me. But, as I entered, a different face looked down from the window. It was the usual Tuesday driver. His shock of red hair and messy beard gave him away immediately. I hesitated a few seconds, as if my mind was playing a trick on me, until the person behind me shoved me forward. I swayed with the tram down the street, my mind wandering. It was weird how thrown I was by her absence. I relied on Stella to always be there. Even though she just drove the tram, I felt more alone than I had in months. I shook my head, trying to get my composure back, but the gnawing feeling in the pit of my stomach wouldn't go away.

At home, I went through the motions of getting ready for a night out; a night out I wasn't particularly interested in partaking in. But I had promised my friends, and I didn't have a good excuse to cancel on such short notice. What was I supposed to say? I can't go out because the girl I pine for wasn't on the tram today. It sounded sad, even to me.

Bar after bar, drink after drink all I could think about was Stella. I was finally ready to talk to her – for the first time since my ticket question. I had it all worked out. The end of the line was only three stops from my house. I was going to wait until the last stop and ask her some banal question, just to buy some time with her. Not a great plan, but it was the best I had come up with. At least now I would have more time to think of something clever to say, something that would make her see how much I liked her. It would just have to wait until after the weekend. If I had waited this long, a few more days weren't going to kill me.

As the shot glass in my hand hit the bar, I was finally starting to feel a bit better. Even drunk, my brain was annoyingly lucid, my sorrows finally starting to drown. I bid my new friends farewell and headed for the reliable old #91 that arrived in mere moments. Late night trams were usually slow and only arrived every 30 minutes. But, as most city dwellers knew, you timed your last drink according to tram times. I could see the lights in the distance as I leaned against the cool plexi-glass of the enclosure. As the tram came skidding to a halt, I could have sworn my drunken eyes were playing tricks. But, it was her behind the glass. Stella – waiting to greet me with her smile. I walked on the tram, feeling my mouth gaping open. I fumbled with my purse to find my ticket, but no matter how much I dug, it refused to be found. She kept her eyes on me, and the few people on the tram were too drunk to care about the delay. She finally motioned me past, her small hand waving me to sit down.

I sat before the tram lurched and wound down the deserted streets. The stops came and went, my fellow tipsy passengers filtered off, finally leaving Stella and me alone. My stop was next, my chances dwindling with each block we passed. When we came to my stop, the tram shimmied to a halt. Stella looked at me; the doors open for me to pass through. But, I didn't move. I just held her gaze, my eyes refusing to leave hers. After a few seconds, she closed the door, and the tram continued down the street past my stop, all the way until the end of the line. I sat there in silence, my stomach flipping over as Stella turned the lights off, putting the tram out of service. Suddenly, the glass door that kept her separated from the rest of the tram opened, and for the first time, I saw all of Stella. She was shorter than me, her long dark hair hanging down her back stopping just above her ass. That horrible uniform didn't do much for her, but her curves were still visible through the cover-all style outfit. It was strange being so close to her, and my whole body registered the proximity. My mouth started moving before I could stop it, the first thing on my mind suddenly coming out of my lips.

'I didn't expect to see you here tonight. You weren't on the 5:17.'

I felt so self conscious, like a schoolgirl. Stella just walked towards me and sat down, leaving very little space between us. The fabric of her uniform brushed against my leg and I could barely breathe.

'Lewis needed to switch. I took his night shift. Lucky for you, I guess.'

Her voice was like honey, seeping into my brain and making me swoon. She slid her hand over my leg, starting at the knee and working her way up. It was such a bold gesture, at least to me. I tried not to look stunned, but I don't think I succeeded. Her hand stopped when it reached the top of my thigh, the hem of my skirt bunching a little under her fingers. I felt a surge of panic run through me, and I started to protest, even though I really didn't want her to stop.

'Stella, what are you doing?'

She smiled and her demeanour was easy and calming.

'Something I think we both want. I realised if I waited for you to make the first move, I'd be waiting for ever.'

Stella leaned closer to me, and my throat felt in danger of closing up. She continued talking, clearly ignoring my nervousness.

'You know, you should really be wearing pantyhose under that skirt. It's a little chilly tonight.'

Before I had the chance to say anything, she kissed me. Her lips were so soft I almost didn't feel them at first. But, her tongue was insistent, swirling into my mouth and taking my breath away. Her hand ran underneath my skirt this time, nudging my thighs apart. But she didn't stop there. Her confident fingers kept moving upwards, until they rested dangerously close to my pussy, making me gasp. I thought she would stop, but she didn't. Her fingers moved again, this time reaching my centre and finding my panties wet.

'But you don't feel chilly at all. In fact, you seem a little hot.'

Stella smiled and ran her finger between my cunt lips, pressing the cotton fabric against my sensitive skin. Her mouth was back on mine, as I urged my hips forward. She was teasing me, pulling away every time I tried to push harder against her hand. I could feel her smile under my lips, knowing she was driving me crazy.

'Stand up.'

Stella's voice echoed off the walls of the tram. The dark was pierced by the nearby streetlight, giving us just enough light to see each other. I stood and walked to the centre of the car, resting my back against the pole busy commuters hung on to all day. She dropped down in front of me, her knees touching my feet. I could barely see the blue of her eyes in the dark. Her hands traced up my thighs, under my skirt and began to tug my panties down. I stepped out of them, moving slowly on my heavy legs. Starting at my knee, Stella's tongue meandered up towards my pussy. I tried to push my hips forward towards her mouth, but she continued on, licking down my other leg. Again, I could feel the smile on her lips, her amusement at my torture. Her fingers found my pussy lips, now naked.

'Stella.'

It was all my mind could manage at that moment. The rest of my thoughts were too jumbled to express. Her thumb pressed my clit, a single finger sliding inside me and pulling all the way back out. She reached her hand to her mouth and licked her finger. A tiny gasp escaped my lips while I watched her. She looked sexier than any woman I had ever seen, even with the ugly uniform hugging her frame. Her moist finger slid back inside me and again came all the way out. While she thrust slowly, she teased the tip of my clit with her soaking wet thumb, applying just the right amount of pressure. Over and over, she plunged her finger inside me and left me empty again. I was practically whimpering for her to speed up, but she kept things at her pace.

'Do you want me to lick that sweet pussy? Is that what all the fuss is about up there?'

She knew exactly what I wanted, and yet still didn't give it to me. I didn't think I could manage to say the words out loud, but looking at her face, I knew she wouldn't continue without them.

'Yes. Please, Stella. Lick my pussy. Stop teasing me.'

She smiled up at me, as she thrust two fingers into my weeping cunt. Finally, after several more agonizingly slow strokes, I felt the warm tip of her tongue wash over me, my clit throbbing at the contact. Her lips closed over my tender flesh, tugging my clit to rapt attention. Her fingers kept moving inside me, the sounds of my moans filling the silence of the tram car. My knees felt like they were ready to give out, so I reached above my head for the handle to steady myself. Her hand held my hip and I let her control everything. She moved me slow, then fast, her fingers furious one minute and plodding the next. Two fingers became three, four, stretching me open further than I had been in months. I could hear her moaning into my cunt, the hum of her lips driving me absolutely mad. Her hand left my hip and I watched as she unzipped her uniform and reached into her own panties.

My orgasm was building inside me, but Stella seemed to know that I was close. She backed off, leaving me restless and edgy. Her fingers were out of my body, their absence teasing and tormenting my empty pussy. As suddenly as she was gone, she was back inside me, making a scream fly out of my mouth. Her tongue attacked me, rubbing over my clit so fast I could barely keep standing. The heat, the explosion of pleasure crashed over me so quickly, I wasn't ready for it. Stella was relentless, keeping me coming longer than I ever had before. I didn't think it was ever going to stop, and I didn't want it to. As far as I was concerned, Stella could keep me like this all night.

Car lights streamed over me and brought me back to reality. The spell was momentarily broken and I collapsed onto the seat closest to me, unable to stand for another second.

Stella sat on the floor, staring at my still twitching body. I felt her hand sweep over my sweaty thigh, sending an aftershock up my spine. Finally, I composed myself and sat up, staring at Stella. She stood, removing her uniform completely. Her silk panties were visibly wet, as she moved her pussy closer to my face. I reached out to touch her soft, tender thigh, the heat of her skin overwhelming me. I looked up at her face and saw her blue eyes burning into me.

'You still need to pay for your trip.'

She smiled, her too-perfect teeth still shining in the dark. I slipped my fingers into the waistband of her thong and slid it down to her ankles. The dark tangle of hair that covered her pussy was matted and wet. I looked up at her blue eyes and smiled. She pulled my mouth close to her pussy and I could smell her sex; raw and pungent. I heard her voice one last time before I began licking her hot pussy.

'There are no free rides, you know.'

Naughty Christmas
by Teri Fritz

SNOWFLAKES SWIRLED PAST THE window as the train pulled into Lübeck train station.

'Looks like we'll have a white Christmas,' the woman in the row across from me was saying. 'It's been ages since we've had one of those. The kids will be pleased.'

I peered through the frosty window at the post-Victorian architecture. The train eased under the curved wrought iron saddle roof and drew to a squeaking halt. The engine let out a hissing sigh and the other passengers hurried to disembark. I stayed seated, adrenaline pumping, mouth dry. Maybe it hadn't been such a good idea to contact my long-lost lover. Maybe I should have just let things be. But it was too late to turn back now, I told myself.

I slipped out of my seat and followed the crowd through to the exit.

My heart thumped as I stepped down on the platform. Thirteen years. I had changed. Had he?

I glanced at the sea of faces, but couldn't find him.

I moved forward, a little uncertain. Shuffling between frolicking children, fussing parents, and raggedy teens, I brushed past a couple with their lips glued together as they tried to chew each other's tongues off.

What if he didn't come?

I brushed my doubts away. If he didn't show up, I'd have a good time at the Christmas market anyway. It was one of the most famous ones in northern Germany. Tourists came from all over to experience the traditional market set in the picturesque medieval square at the heart of the old town.

The sweetness of a rose invaded my nostrils. The headiness brought back an instant flood of memories.

'Andre!'

He pulled me into his arms slowly, his eyes burning into mine, daring me to resist. I knew he'd release me if I protested. I didn't. He dipped his head to brush his lips against my throat, a gesture more intimate than a kiss on the lips, I realised, shivering.

The scent of tobacco and spice clung to the green jacket of his uniform.

'You're on duty?'

'Just got off.'

'Aren't you tired?'

'Never too tired for you. Come.'

He placed his hand in the small of my back and led me up the wooden stairs to the front of the station.

The heat of his palm seared my backbone, sent tingles along my spine. I felt my knees waver, but his hand on my elbow steadied me as we wove our way through the masses, past the conference centre and the leaning brick gate called the Holstentor.

'The town has changed,' I said, looking around ostensibly.

'Some parts have,' he agreed. His green eyes glittered at me. 'You look the same, a little thinner maybe?'

'Could be,' I shrugged. I glanced at the boats docked on the banks of the Wakenitz. That hadn't changed. 'It's been a long time.'

I didn't mention that he had changed. I could hardly remember what he'd looked like in real life. The photo of him in his UN regulation uniform with the blue ring around the sleeve was the only memento I had left of him. It had been taken by an official photographer at the scene of a bombing in Bosnia. And I had kept it in the back of my address book. Years after I'd given up all hope of ever seeing him again, I would still pull it out occasionally and dream. The memory of his lips on my body haunted me, the way he'd trembled in my hands, how he'd flipped me masterfully to penetrate me from behind. My phantom lover had followed me for years. Now the man stood before me in the flesh again.

The market square before the Marienkirche cathedral was packed with eager visitors. Quaint wooden stalls exuded a mixture of sweet, spicy and savoury smells. Cinnamon and cloves in mulled wine, the chocolaty flavour of homemade marzipan, sugar-coated almonds, and peppermint candy canes melded into the typical Christmas magic.

'Hot mulled wine?' he asked, pausing at one of the stands with huge, steaming copper vats of the German specialty.

'No, thanks, I'd prefer mead,' I said.

He got himself a malty pint of dark beer and handed me the mead in a ceramic medieval mug.

'It's way too early for alcohol,' I protested feebly, sipping the hot liquid.

'Live dangerously!' he teased.

We found a place to rest on a table. The crowd was howling Christmas songs.

'O Tannenbaum, O Tannenbaum, wie schön sind deine Blätter.'

'So tell me,' he began, just as I opened my mouth to ask how life had been after Bosnia.

We both laughed.

'You first,' he said.

'No, you tell me about your life,' I insisted.

So he told me about his mum who was in a senior residence in Hamburg, about his promotion at the police academy, and his passion for rock climbing.

'No more sky diving?' I asked.

'No. It's too expensive for a poor policeman like me. Besides, I don't fit with the crowd any more. How about you?'

'I never got around to it again after we, after the last time with you,' I said. 'But this mead has whet my appetite. Shall we get something to eat?' I didn't want to talk about my life.

'As you wish,' he nodded, bowing forward slightly.

After strolling past the rows of stalls we found a couple of good offers. We munched on roasted goose with cranberry chutney, fresh French crepes with chocolate sauce and washed it down with warm red wine.

Andre hummed along to the Christmas tunes and pressed his body against mine. My breath quickened. Almost imperceptibly, his lips brushed my ear. 'Shall we get out of here?' he suggested.

I nodded and followed him down the cobble-stoned centre of the city.

'Oh, the fairytale forest,' I squealed, stalling for time. Suddenly, I wasn't sure I could face him in the close quarters of his apartment. I dragged him through the enclosed area with fairytale floats sponsored by charitable organisations.

'I love Snow White,' I raved in front of the stall with a horde of dwarfs.

His hands rested on my shoulders kneading away the tension.

'It's a lot more gemutlich at my place,' he suggested. 'Why do I get the feeling you're avoiding it?'

I turned to him. 'You always could see right through me,' I admitted. 'I'm not sure I–'

'We won't do anything you don't want, I promise.'

I stared at him for a moment. That was the problem. I was afraid we might do something I did want, even though I knew I shouldn't. But I went with him anyway.

His flat was a fully modernised split-level unit

overlooking the historical Hugstrasse. The warm wood and panelled floors contrasted with the metallic smoothness of modern equipment.

I ran my hand over the familiar escritoire in the corner.

'You still have this?' I marvelled.

'Some things don't change,' he answered, taking my coat and hanging it on the wardrobe hook.

'Coffee?'

I nodded and moved to the couch as he went to the kitchen area to prepare it.

I flipped through the photo album under the coffee table. Photos of him from a peacekeeping mission in Kosovo. I had kept one of those on my mantelpiece for years before I finally gave up hope.

'Why did you stop writing?' I burst out. 'I thought you were dead.' It should have sounded casual, funny, but it had too much of an edge. As I spoke, my fingers traced the face of a sloe-eyed Slavic beauty.

He didn't answer. Instead he came back with two steaming cups. I cradled the coffee he'd pressed into my hand, admiring the Miro painting on the wall. We had that in common. Our taste in art had always matched.

'One thing led to another,' he said, shrugging. 'And besides, you were the one who got married.'

I bent my head at that, my hair falling across my face to shield me from his accusing eyes. He wasn't letting me off that easily. He raised my chin with a knuckle, brooking no resistance, forcing me to meet his eyes.

'Are you happy?'

I looked away. 'Yes,' I stammered. Sometimes I was. Karl and I had a good relationship. Companionable. But we didn't share the passion I'd known with Andre. If he looked in my eyes, he would know.

He raised my chin again and searched my eyes.

Then his lips sank and captured mine. He waited, leaving the rest up to me.

I wanted to resist, but the hunger welled up inside me. I kissed him back, opened my lips to him and my heart, letting all the longing and worry of 13 years show. I pressed my breasts against the firmness of his chest, struggling to eliminate the space between us. He obliged me, flipping me under him on the couch with a skilful half roll.

His body crushed me into the cushions.

My fingers combed through his hair, enjoying the fuzzy crew cut, soft as down.

We rolled off the sofa; his body shielded mine as we landed with a thump on the floor. I tugged at his shirt, freeing it from his trousers. My fingers fumbled with his belt, greedily grabbed the hard shaft that rose up to greet me. It was my turn to hold his eyes. He watched me as I dipped my tongue to him, lunging forward, upward to meet my lips. I closed around him and sucked his sweetness, savouring the dribble of moisture that glistened on the tip of his cock.

He buried his hands in my hair and dragged me up to meet his lips, plundering my mouth, demanding his due.

Then he flipped me over and raised my backside, pulling my jeans off my hips and ripping the lace panties impatiently.

'Wait,' I protested weakly.

He paused, his cock straining against my hot, moist flesh.

'A condom? I don't have anything, do you?'

He slapped my bottom in response and went to the bedroom, returning with a box of lubricated condoms.

I smiled up at him saucily as we shared the task of rolling the protective sheath over his stiff penis. He groaned. I lingered over the smoothing of it. He bent his head and caught a nipple between his teeth, biting down wickedly.

'Ah,' I squealed in protest. He nuzzled me again, stroking my other breast while sucking and nipping at the bruised nipple. He ended with a tantalising kiss, blowing air over it to soothe me, but it only made me hotter.

'Please,' I whispered.

He spun me around and plunged into me from behind.

It was like I remembered. He stretched me, pounded me, his thighs slapping against mine as he held me steady. My head was buried in the cushions we'd displaced from the sofa. A moan gurgled in my throat. But before I could let it out, he flipped me over, stretching my legs and grinding his hips between them.

I shuddered, and opened my mouth to scream, but he swallowed the sound, filling me with the taste of mulled wine and coffee. And just when I reached the edge of my tolerance, he changed positions again.

This time I was on top. It took me a moment to gauge the situation, and reorient myself. I began to move my hips slowly, circling, swooping, withdrawing, plunging, sucking him into me as I set the rhythm.

'Uh,' he grunted. 'That feels good.'

I blushed and let my hair hide my pleasure. I pressed his shoulders down and arched my back, riding like a hellion, enjoying my dominance, glorying in the power of it until I finally collapsed on him, losing consciousness for a moment.

His lips nudged my ear, his fingers stroked my face gently, but I was lost to the world. After an eternity, I regained consciousness and sat up groggily. He was watching me, his dick still hard, a little forlorn after being abandoned.

'Poor boy,' I cooed. Our eyes met and held each other as I snaked my tongue out to taste his belly button. He jerked upwards, trembling under my hands. I smiled.

The sight of his uniform discarded on the floor gave me an idea. I trailed a fingernail over his chest and clambered over him to rummage in his things. I found the handcuffs easily enough and waved them over his nose, an eyebrow raised.

He grinned back at me. I found the key, opened the

cuffs and snapped them over his wrists, chaining him to the head of the bed. I slipped on his jacket and set his cap on my head at a jaunty angle.

'OK, prisoner,' I snapped. 'You're accused of sexual abandonment.' I made a show of pacing in front of the bed, slapping his baton in my palm.

His eyes watched in muted anticipation as I trailed the baton over his chest.

'Do you know how much I suffered, wondering what had happened to you, if some terrorist insurgent had blown your head off, or worse, your balls? Not knowing if I'd ever see you again, or if you were even alive?' I used the heavy stick to prod him in the ribs then push up his chin. I lowered my voice to a sinister growl and leaned over him, so my breath fanned his face.

'It was cruel and unusual punishment. How do you plead?'

'Yes, please, fuck me,' he growled.

I couldn't help but laugh. That was the extent of my need for domination. I tossed the baton aside. Then I swung my legs over him, holding him captive between my thighs as I explored the sensitive tips of his nipples with my nails and tongue. He bolted and strained beneath me.

I went down on him as he watched me, my fingers circling his shaft while my tongue lathed kisses on the tip of his cock. He was making tortured noises, writhing, wriggling and bucking beneath me. I grabbed his buttocks and buried my face in his groin as he pumped his juices into my mouth. His head fell back and he shouted his pleasure. Then silence.

'Are you OK?' I asked shyly when he opened his eyes again.

He smiled drowsily and wiggled his imprisoned arms.

'Oh, sorry,' I grinned. I scrambled to get the keys, then paused wickedly above him.

'Hmm, maybe I'll keep you prisoner and use you for my

pleasure so you'll never be able to leave me again.'

'It's you who'll leave me,' he contradicted.

I opened the cuffs guiltily and rubbed the blood back into his wrists, placing a kiss on the spot where his pulse beat, letting my tongue taste the rhythm of his heart.

'You don't have to go back to him. Tell him it's over,' he said, pushing a strand of my hair back and tucking it behind my ear.

'I can't,' I said. 'I promised. In sickness and in health, 'til death do us part.'

'But you don't love him,' Andre snarled, grabbing my shoulders, shaking me so hard I thought my head would fall off.

It was true. I loved Andre. After all these years, we still moved together as if we were made for each other. Like Ginger and Fred, Liz and Richard, or Bogey and Bacall, all those other classic storybook lovers.

But there was Karl.

'I can't,' I repeated and rushed for the bathroom.

I hid my tears in the stream of hot water that lashed my skin in the shower. I was careful not to let my hair get wet. My fingers parted the flesh of my cunt, feeling the tenderness, the sticky evidence of our pairing, the heat.

Suddenly, I felt him behind me. His fingers brushed mine aside insistently. 'Let me,' he said.

I let him. He rubbed the soap between my legs, up my belly, massaging my breasts, lingering at my neck, then he turned me around to face him, hoisted my hips against his and pressed me into the cold tiles.

'My hair,' I protested. 'I don't want to get my hair wet.'

It was a stupid thing to say, and the way he looked at me confirmed it. He planted his legs wide and turned the head of the shower aside so the water hit me at chest level. Our bodies slapped and slipped against each other, and I tossed my head back, not knowing if the moans were coming from my throat or his. Not caring any more about my hair.

Afterwards, he let me down gently. He turned off the water and reached for a fluffy, white towel. As he wrapped me in the soft terry material, I leaned against him and rested my head on his chest.

He stroked my hair and pressed my face against his flesh. My tongue flicked out to taste him. I couldn't resist.

'I have to go. I'll miss my train.'

He didn't answer, but his hands paused for a second before he finished rubbing and patting the water from my skin.

'You gotta do what you gotta do,' he murmured.

I finished dressing in silence while he watched. He had wrapped a towel around his waist, but I could see the muscles rippling on his abdomen, not an ounce of fat to spare. He hadn't gotten out of shape. I could still feel the firmness of him against my softness.

I felt him all the way back home to my clueless husband.

'Had a good time with Andrea?' Karl asked, barely looking up from the computer screen.

'Yes,' I said, not bothering to kiss him. He didn't notice, too preoccupied with the game.

I escaped to the bedroom to replace the torn knickers I'd left at Andre's place. I pulled on my fluffy bathrobe and inspected the bite mark on my left breast. Karl wouldn't notice, but a thrill of guilt coursed through me and I touched myself, remembering ...

'Would you like me to make you a cup of hot cocoa?' Karl offered, appearing in the bedroom door.

'Oh,' I stammered, pulling my robe closed hastily. 'That would be nice.' I followed him to the kitchen.

'Did you find what you wanted at the Christmas market?'

'Yes, but it's a surprise,' I said.

I didn't know if I would have the guts to tell him. How do you tell your partner you've betrayed him with someone else? I need time, I told myself. My timing couldn't have been worse. Finding a long-lost lover online might not have been such a good idea after all. It had seemed brilliant at the time, the Google search, the thrill of seeing his name, the first email, the first telephone contact after 13 years. Then making the date to meet at one of our old haunts: the Christmas market in Lübeck. Falling into incredible sex ... And now?

I don't want to hurt Karl. But living a lie will hurt us both. I don't know how I'll survive this Christmas, the family festivities, his stepdad's awkward advances, his mum's critical looks, all the while with Andre on my mind. But I think I'll wait until New Year's. It's only a couple of weeks away.

And then I'll decide whether to confess to Karl and see what he says. Until then, it's my wicked little secret. I can't help but grin when I think of it. It makes me warm all over to remember how it felt.

Andre and I may never get back together forever, but I'm glad we could be together just one more time. His arms and lips erased the trauma and worry of missing him all those years. And even if I've ruined my marriage, it was worth it somehow. I feel like a new woman, no longer haunted by the shadows of the past.

I've had myself a naughty little Christmas, but I don't care what Santa says. What was that saying I read somewhere: Good girls go to heaven, bad girls have fun?

Whatever happens, I am determined to make the best of life from now on. It'll be a Happy New Year for a happy new me.

Xcite

Xcite Books help make loving better
with a wide range of erotic books,
eBooks, adult products
and dating sites.

www.xcitebooks.com

facebook

Sign-up to our Facebook page
for special offers and free gifts!